FROM SUITS TO KILTS

The Time Orb Series Book I

CALLIE BERKHAM

From Suits to Kilts:
The Time Orb Series Book I
Copyright © Callie Berkham 2019
Cover design by Gabrielle Prendergast
Published 2021 by DCF Books
ISBN: 978-0-9945011-1-0
DCF Books
CPA Calcium, 4545 Flinders Highway, Calcium, Qld, 4816
ABN 36069542904

Abby stopped the small rental car and fell back against her seat. She was late. Her three siblings would have already arrived home, and they would want to hear about her wedding plans. She snorted and squeezed the steering wheel. There would be no wedding. They didn't need to know the details.

She let out a loud sigh, and stepping out of the car, gazed at the house she had grown up in. She bit her bottom lip as memories flashed through her mind of laughing children chasing their father around the house. Although times like that were few and far between, Abby had to admit, she and her siblings had happy times growing up.

She peered up at the massive white brick building, a shiver running up her backbone.

The few occasions she had been home before her parents died, she hadn't felt anything unusual. This time, though, her senses were heightened, as if something wasn't quite right. She tipped her head and took in the entire building. Maybe she was just feeling uneasy because this was the first family get-together since their parents' fatal accident. The first time she, her sisters, and her brother would be home at the same time. The first time without their parents either about to go somewhere or coming from somewhere.

Once she'd pulled on her suit jacket, she slung her overnight bag over her shoulder. She had worn her favorite black pants suit for the trip to cheer herself up, but she regretted the decision. She felt overdressed. She twisted her hair into a spiral ponytail and clipped her auburn locks to the back of her head.

Drawing in a deep breath, she stepped up onto the porch and rested her hand on one of the heavy oak doors for a moment to center herself.

Physically, the house didn't appear any different from the last time she saw it, but emotionally, it had her nerves aquiver. She didn't like feeling apprehensive. She was usually the one who had it all together, the person her younger siblings looked to for strength when they were beaten down by life. Maybe she was hungry. After all, she hadn't eaten since that horrid snack on the plane. She hoped someone had made dinner.

She unlocked the door and slowly opened it inward, stepping over the threshold. Her shoulders relaxed as she spotted her brother's paintings hanging on cream walls. Her eyes widened as her gaze caught on a painting with a black stallion rearing at the edge of a cliff, with a magnificent multicolored sunset filling the background. She knew immediately it was her brother's work, but she hadn't seen this one before and wondered when Garrett had hung the painting.

Before she took another step, Maxine swooped down the curving staircase.

Abby eyed her younger sister's familiar blue jeans and low shoes, but her eyes lingered on the soft lemon shirt for a second. She thought it suited her sister's dark looks to perfection, and it was much more feminine than the black or gray shirts she usually wore.

"Max!" Abby rushed forward and hugged her. Max, being shorter, wrapped her arms around her back and gave her a quick squeeze before letting go.

Taking Max's arm in hers, Abby leaned back. "I love that shirt."

"Thanks."

Max allowed the show of affection for as long as it took to walk into the dining room then she moved away. Abby scanned the room. The table had been set for four, but no one else was there. "Where is everybody?"

"They'll be here soon enough. Garrett might not talk much, but he's a darn good cook."

The sisters sat down in the same Elizabethan chairs they had used since childhood.

Max held the coffee pot up to her. "You still take sugar?"

Abby grinned. "Yeah, I'm still not sweet enough."

Max laughed. "You'll never be sweet enough."

They sipped from their mugs in comfortable silence, and after a while, Abby eyed her sister. "I've missed you."

Max smiled. "I've missed you too."

"How do you like your work at the veterinary clinic? Is Rowan a good vet?"

"He's the greatest and I love it, at least I love helping the vet with the horses and of course the dogs and cats are wonderful." She made a face and shivered. "Not the mice and rats though. Why on earth would anyone want to keep a rat for a pet?"

"They're supposed to be quite intelligent."

"So Rowan keeps telling me."

Although Abby was interested in Max's career change, she really wanted to know how her sister was doing in the wake of their parent's deaths.

"I can't believe it's been a year since Mom and Dad died," Abby said, looking into her coffee cup. "You know Izzy's been spending a lot of time with me this last year? She took Mom and Dad's deaths badly, but I don't know what Garrett is feeling. He's so hard to read." Abby smiled. "Maybe having all of us here it will help them move forward."

"They'll be fine. How are you, though?"

Abby's smile wavered and she scratched a small itch on her neck. "I'm okay. What about you?"

Max shrugged and leaned back. "People die. It's not as if we were close to them. They were never around, always too busy with their dumb old bones or fifteenth-century jugs."

She stood up, strolled to the mantel, and held up their parents' last find, waving the jug in the air. "What good is a fifteenth-century jug, anyway? To look at? To always be on edge in case someone broke the stupid thing?" She threw Abby a grin and bobbed, pretending to drop it.

"Put it back, Max. I think it's beautiful, and you know it's worth a fortune."

"Yeah, worth so much more than four rowdy kids, huh?" Max put it back and plonked down onto her chair.

Abby couldn't say anything in response to that. Max was right. Their parents lived and breathed archaeology. She understood their passion—after all, she was an ardent historian herself. But why they bothered to have four children was beyond her. They had spent months at a time away, tracking down old stuff. Even when they were at home, they spent all their time in either the attic or the basement, reviewing and cataloging their finds, so they might as well have been traveling.

The earlier memory of her father came to mind, and Abby said, "We did have some happy times, though, didn't we?"

Max shrugged again. "I stopped in Brukstoe on the way here, and Ellie Hadden, you remember her? Anyway, she told me there's a new spa open at Hadden Inn, and it's supposed to have all the latest stuff. She thought you'd like to know."

Abby laughed. She, her sisters, and Ellie had spent most of their older teenage years either in beauty parlors in Brukstoe or, when they could swing it, in spas in Chicago. Of course, if Abby's parents hadn't felt guilty for the lack of time they spent with their daughters, the girls would never have been able to afford such luxuries.

Izzy loved the spas and parlors as much as Abby did, and although Max always said she only went for the company, Abby was sure she enjoyed them too.

Even now, Abby spent time in any spa that she could find. They relaxed her, and she found them rejuvenating like nothing else. She had decided long ago she would open her very own spa one day and was excited that Ellie Haddon had done just that. "I'll ring her first thing tomorrow."

Out of nowhere, a shiver passed down Abby's spine, and she looked around to find a reason. The windows were open but there wasn't a breeze blowing the curtains, and it was a warm day. She looked down at the floor. They were never allowed in the basement when their parents were alive, but now there was nothing stopping her from having a look. She looked up and found Max staring at her.

Her sister grinned. "You can go down there anytime."

"Have you?"

Max shook her head. "Nope, not yet. I wanted someone with me. Don't know why, but I just did."

"Yeah, I get that. I do too."

"How about we wait till everyone's here, and we can all go down together."

Abby wasn't sure the others would want to, but it wasn't a bad idea.

"Abby," Izzy called out as she swept into the dining room.

Abby stood up as her youngest sister paused by the fireplace. "Hang on," she said, pushing her long blonde hair from her face as she plucked her cell phone from her bag.

Watching her sister, Abby smiled. Izzy was always girly, and today she was no different with her pretty blue-and-white printed dress with flute sleeves and a ruffled hem.

A frown flashed between Izzy's blue eyes as she checked her cell.

"Bad news?" Abby asked.

"No, everything's fine." She hurried forward and gave Abby a quick hug. "I better tell Garrett you're here."

And with that, Izzy nearly ran back out the door. The girl was always rushing about as if she would never have time to accomplish all the things she wanted to do in her lifetime. Even as a young child, she never walked if she could run.

Since their parents' deaths, Izzy seemed to be even busier every second of the day. Even when she had visited Abby, she either shut herself in her room to write her novels or constantly talked and texted on her phone.

Abby spotted Garrett on the threshold holding a large tray of roast meat and vegetables. As he walked into the room, Izzy ducked past him with a jug of gravy.

Abby waited for Garrett to put the tray on the table and held out her arms. He hesitated, and her heart sank at the thought he might not accept the offer. However, he wrapped his arms around her, squeezed for less than a second, then let go and moved to sit down at the table.

She grimaced inwardly. Her little brother, dressed in his usual leather jacket, white T-shirt, and tight blue jeans, was becoming more and more alienated from the family. He never showed up for get-togethers anymore. She had to stop herself from pushing his black hair from over his eye. His nose was still a little bent from colliding with the fist of a so-called friend, but she was thankful it looked no worse than the last time she had seen him. No new injuries meant he had hopefully not been in too many more fights.

She gazed at him, trying to see under the armor he'd slowly built around himself his entire life.

As Max and Izzy filled their plates with food, the scent of rosemary and garlic wafted to Abby's nose and her stomach grumbled. Her gaze drifted from the platter to her sisters, and she spotted a box at the end of the long table.

"What's that?" she asked no one in particular.

"Don't know," Max said. "It was here when we got here. There's a note from the lawyer that we couldn't open it until we all were together."

"I wonder why Carter didn't meet with us himself," Abby said, still eyeing the box. "I haven't seen or spoken to him since he read the wills after the funeral."

"Me either," Max said.

"He was really upset at the funeral," Izzy added.

"Well, he would be," Max said. "He was Dad's friend since grade school, and then his confidant and lawyer their entire adult lives."

Garrett put his empty glass down with a thud. "I didn't say anything before because it might have been my imagination, but did any of you notice how cagey Carter acted when we asked questions about Mom and Dad and what they did? It seemed to me like he was hiding something."

"Now that you bring it up, I did notice that," Max said. "But I thought he was just grieving like we all were and didn't want to talk about anything personal."

"That's what I thought too," Izzy said.

"I didn't notice anything different about him. Oh, he was upset—we all were—but he seemed like the same old Carter to me," Abby said with a shrug.

She stood up and strode over to the package. "Maybe that's why he isn't here now. He was obviously keeping whatever's in this box from us." She stroked the cardboard top. "Let's see what's in it that Carter couldn't have shown us a year ago."

Izzy swallowed. "Maybe it holds something special for each of us. Maybe they left a personal letter just for us."

Garrett sniffed in disdain. "You really think they took the time to write us a love letter?"

"I didn't mean a love letter, but yeah, something to let us know how much they cared for us." Izzy pursed her lips and flicked her blonde hair over her shoulder. "Why not?"

Abby put a hand up to stop their arguing. "Why don't we just find out?"

As she said the last words, she was already tearing at the cardboard box. She pulled out a long, black cloak. "That's strange."

Izzy hurried to her side and pulled out an envelope. Using her fingernail to open it and unfold a sheet of paper, she silently read it.

Abby put the cloak over the back of a chair. "Well? What does it say?"

"It's from Mom and Dad," Izzy said, her eyes wide with excitement. "But written in Dad's hand. He says, *If you're reading this, it's been twelve months since both of us or the surviving parent died. Please know we have loved you all and regret not spending more time with you as you grew into the wonderful adults we know you now are.*

"*Read the journals in the box and keep the artifact safe. Be careful. It is a . . .*"—she paused and gaped at her brother and sisters in turn before continuing—"*time device.*"

Abby snatched the letter from her. She quickly scanned the words and discovered that was exactly what her father had written. She snorted. "Dad does say that."

"Ooh, a mystery," Izzy said, looking around as if she thought Indiana Jones would barge in at any moment.

Garrett had joined them at the end of the table and plucked a white orb from the box. It was clean and new looking, with gold filigree leaves circling the middle.

"*Time device* must be some sort of code name for this," he said, turning the orb in his hands. He waved it about and made ghostly noises. "It's probably a portal to the dark side. We'd better be careful, or we'll have poltergeists swarming all over the house."

Max laughed.

Abby chuckled. "I doubt we're in any danger. They wouldn't do that to us." She gazed at the orb and shivered. "Would they?"

CHAPTER 2

A bby trailed her hands down her face, trying to rid herself of the feeling of dread that had firmly planted itself in her chest.

Max glanced at Abby and raised a dark eyebrow at Garrett. "Stop trying to spook us. It's probably just another four-thousand-year-old vase."

Abby shushed her and gave the letter to Garrett, saying, "They say they hope the piece will bring fulfillment to our lives."

"Now they care about enriching our lives." Garrett sniffed.

Izzy pulled out a stack of notebooks and placed them on the table beside the box. "These are their journals."

Max squeezed between Garrett and Izzy and began shuffling through the journals.

Not bothering to move aside to give his sister better access, Garrett narrowed his eyes and wrinkled his nose at the pile as if they smelled like fresh horse manure.

He continued to read the letter aloud. *"We have always been proud of each and every one of you, and we couldn't have been more pleased that you are all successful, intelligent adults."*

"Sure. As long as we stayed out of their hair," Max mumbled.

Garrett chuckled, but Izzy looked at her with wide, sad eyes. Abby stopped herself from going to her and comforting her. She knew Izzy detested it when Max or Garrett blamed their parents for not spending more time with them. Izzy was always quick to make excuses for them.

Continuing, Garrett read, *"The journals will clarify what we have been doing all these years and why our work kept us away from home so often. Please do not meddle with the time device until you have read every journal."*

"Fair enough," Max said, and handed one of the books to Garrett.

Abigail thought for a moment her brother wasn't going to take it, but he begrudgingly accepted it. He held the journal away from his body as if he were scared a giant spider would crawl out of the pages and bite him.

Max let out a laugh. "So, we finally find out what they've been doing all these years instead of, like, raising us?"

Izzy gave Max a slight shake of her head. "Our parents may not have been with us every moment while we were growing up, but they did love us."

She gazed at Abby for reinforcement, so Abby said, "We know they loved us, don't we, Maxine? Garrett?"

"I guess," Max said.

Garrett's bottom lip dropped. "If you say so."

Abby glanced at the orb and a thrill of excitement pushed away the dread in her chest. Even without understanding exactly what it was, she knew with certainty there was something strange about the orb. For starters, it looked brand new. It was clean and smooth, and white as a fresh sheet of paper.

Her parents hated modern ornaments; their idea of decorating was displaying the oldest stuff they could find in whatever condition they found it. Her mother had often said a chip here and there added character to an item. The white orb had no character whatsoever, even the gold filigree appeared newly made. It was the opposite of anything her parents would have wanted in their house.

Her eyes swept over her siblings. Garrett had his bored look firmly in place, and Max was still wrinkling her nose as if she couldn't care less. Izzy was the only other person who looked intrigued as she gazed in awe at the ornament.

Abby eyed the orb and drew in a deep breath. "Maybe we'll find out what they meant by *a time device* if we actually read the journals."

Izzy was already reading, and Max plucked a book off the table.

Garrett glanced at the journal he'd left on the table and stared at Abby.

"Come on, Garrett. This could be interesting," Abby said. "Think about it. Something important must have had them traipsing all about the globe instead of parenting us." He picked up the journal and Abby hid a smile. At least he was listening.

"If I'm honest and not letting my nasty side out, I do believe they loved us." Max huffed.

Abby continued. "Remember how they made it a point to always be here for our birthdays? And remember how much fun we had chasing Dad around the house? He always let us take turns in catching him, so we must have meant something to them for them to do that." Gazing at each of them, she raised her eyebrows in question.

"Maybe," Max said.

Garrett flipped his book open. "Fine."

Abby shook her head as she absently flipped through the typed journal. "Let's just read what they have to say. But first,

I've got to eat some of this wonderful food Garrett made for us."

They all agreed and sat back down in their seats to eat.

After she was well and truly sated, Abby moved her plate and began flipping through the journal. Her eyes caught a bolded sentence.

Naseby, Northamptonshire, England, 1645.

She knew immediately that was the site of an important battle during England's First Civil War. She loved reading about historical events in her free time—though, to be honest, teaching a group of rowdy eight-year-olds all subjects didn't leave her with time for much beyond marking homework and organizing the next day's class schedule. She sat back and continued reading, curious about why her parents had included that particular event in the journal.

The entry was an account of the defeat of the royalists by the parliamentarians. The strange thing was that it was written as though her parents had been there for the events. Her mother wrote from her heart about how she cried at the carnage and how her father risked his life to recover an artifact on the field only to have it disappear before his very eyes.

She read on and gasped. A photograph of her parents dressed in the garb of that time and holding what she was sure was King Charles' chief military advisor's feathered hat was pasted at the bottom of the page. From what she knew of England 1645, her parents' outfits were more than knockoff costumes. And the events taking place around them, paired with their detailed written accounts, were not what a normal archeologist would be documenting. Plus, the type of photography hadn't been invented at that time.

It was almost as if . . . but no. It was too ridiculous to think that her parents had actually *been there*.

Still, they would either have had to be several hundred years old or been able to travel back in time.

She scoffed, trying to convince herself it was crazy to even entertain the idea of time travel. The white orb caught her eye, and she found herself momentarily captivated by the opaque surface. Something about the orb was definitely not normal, and she wondered briefly how it was connected to the journals.

Shaking her head to clear it of the absurd notion that time travel was possible, Abby glanced up at her siblings. They were also reading intently, and by the covert looks at the orb, they seemed to be having a similar experience.

Max had a deep frown embedded between her perfectly arched brows, and her mouth hovered somewhere between a sneer and a disbelieving smile.

Izzy's eyes were wide and excited as they scanned the words in the book, and Garrett's hands seemed to have a barely noticeable tremor to them as he continued flipping through the journal.

"This could be a plot for one of my novels," Izzy said. "Or with the amount of info here, I could write a never-ending series. I guess I get my imagination from our parents."

Abby smiled at her. "I guess we all get something from them. They've written up the history of their destinations perfectly, just like I would have, and look, Max." Abby flipped to a picture of the first-ever games in Olympia. "These sections are for you. They were as obsessed with sports as you are."

Max made a face. "I'm not obsessed. I'm merely interested is all."

Izzy laughed. "Yeah, right. That's why you have a hundred dans or whatever black belts in every martial art ever taught."

She laughed. "I'm only sixth dan in karate, silly."

"That's still pretty cool," Abby said.

Garrett turned his journal to the side and admired the middle pages. Abby hadn't seen him so animated since he was a child. He turned the book around so they could all see the magnificent drawing of a horse and wagon. "Check out the drawings. I guess I get my art skills from them as well."

He glanced at Abby, and she thought just for a second that he was going to smile, but instead, his face shut down and he leaned back against the wall and returned to flipping through the pages.

Max threw her journal on the table. "This reminds me of when I was training. My mentor taught me not to believe all I read or saw. There's always a logical explanation for everything."

Keeping her gaze on the orb, Abby stood up and moved toward it. If only it were true. Time travel, a historian's dream come true. "I don't know, Max. I think the least we can do is read these journals and try to keep an open mind. Mom and Dad left them for us, and they would have expected us to at least believe them." She waved her hand over the discarded notebooks piled on the coffee table. "The photographs could have been doctored, but I doubt it."

Garrett had artistic eyes. If anyone could spot a fake, it would be him. "Garrett? What do you make of the photos?"

He glanced up with a slight frown as if processing what Abby had asked, and then peered at a page in his journal. "If they were manipulated, then I'd like to meet whoever did it. They're perfect."

"See?" Abby said to Max.

"But," Garrett jumped in, "that doesn't mean I believe they time traveled. They could have dressed up and hired actor lookalikes for the pictures."

Izzy gazed at Garrett. "I think they're authentic. Look at the backgrounds. There's no way they would have had all that built just for a photograph."

Garrett scoffed. "You just want them to be real." He continued reading, already finished with the conversation.

Max huffed and also went back to her journal.

The doorbell rang, and Garrett raised his brows at his sisters.

Abby shrugged. "Might be Carter." She rushed to the front door and swung it open. Before she could focus on who it was, a voice shrilled.

"Abby! How are you?"

Abby glanced over her shoulder at Garrett, who had followed her. He waved his hands as if to tell Abby not to let her in.

"Ah, good, good. What brings you here?"

"I wanted to see all of you." Bree tipped her head back, her green eyes rolling to the side to indicate the car parked in the drive. "And I'd love a strong coffee. I'm beat."

Abby frowned. Why would Bree turn up at that moment?

Garrett grunted and, nudging Abby out of the way, pulled the door back. "It's good to see you, Bree."

Bree gave Garrett a hug. "And you, little cousin."

Garrett, never one for physical shows of affection, pushed her away from him.

Abby was still organizing her thoughts. Brianna had spent a lot of time with them during their childhood. Her own parents died when she was a teenager, and she lived with her paternal grandmother. Her mother was Abby's mother's twin sister, Patricia. Abby rubbed her forehead. Of course, Mom would never keep secrets from her twin. But did they let Bree in on the secret? She eyed Brianna who was giggling at Garrett.

"I was worried about you all." Her flaming-red hair bounced as she bobbed in a knowing way. "And when Carter told me you were all back together here, I just had to come." She gave them both a wry grimace. "I guess it's all too much to take in a short time."

"Huh?" Abby said, feeling stupid the moment the grunt

left her mouth. Bree did know, and now she was laughing at them.

"What do you mean by that?" Garrett said.

"Are we going to stand out here all day, or are you going to invite me in?"

Shaking her head, Abby stepped back and sent a move-out-of-the-way look to Garrett. "Come in."

Max and Izzy jumped up as the trio walked back into the dining room.

"Bree!" Izzy rushed to her and gave her a hug. "I didn't know you were coming!"

Max said, "I didn't either."

Bree grinned at Max and gave her a quick hug. "I've missed you guys."

"So, what are you doing here?" Max asked.

Bree flicked her red locks over her shoulder and let out a loud sigh. "I might as well just come out and tell you. Carter told me your parents wanted me to be here, and yes, I know all about their time traveling." She grinned. "Apparently, I'm supposed to make sure you all believe it."

"Why would our parents tell you and not us?" Abby asked.

"They didn't. Mom told me a long time ago. She also told me she made Aunt Di promise to take me back in time with them." Her eyes teared up. "They were supposed to take me this year."

"What a load of rubbish," Garrett said, plonking down in his chair.

Bree swiped her eyes with the side of her hands. "You don't have to believe me, I'm just telling you what I was told." She pointed to the tray of food. "So, is there any coffee left?"

"Of course," Abby said, and poured her a mug of espresso. She wasn't sure she believed everything Bree had said either but decided they could talk about it more later. "Have you read their journals?"

"I haven't, but I'd love to." Bree sipped her coffee and picked up the black cloak. "This is neat. It looks like it'd fit you, Abby. Why don't you try it on?"

Abby put on the cloak. It was too warm for inside the house, but it was soft and snuggly.

Bree held out the orb and handed it to Abby. "Do you think this is the time device?"

Abby's hands shook with excitement as she took the orb. "I have no idea." She tipped her head to the side. The top was out of alignment with the bottom. She twisted it so the gold leaf design matched up perfectly. *What if it was—*

She never finished the thought before her fingers tingled and a jolt of electricity rushed up her arms. A sudden rushing in her ears drowned out the sound of her siblings' chatter. She squeezed her eyes shut and tried to take note of the sensations. The feeling of falling was strangely exhilarating until she realized that the landing might hurt. Before she could worry much about it, there was a slowing sensation. She felt more like she was floating gently downward. Her feet touched solid ground, and she opened her eyes.

CHAPTER 3

I ain MacLaren threw down his musket and roared like a lion. Prince Charles, the king Charles Edward Stuart, the rightful king of England and Scotland, the man Iain wanted to fight for, the man he was willing to die for, had forsaken the Jacobites.

Cumberland's troops had outmanned and out-armed the Jacobites. The perpetually wet Drumossie Moor had become even more sodden by the blood of his clansmen, countrymen, and their allies.

Had Bonnie Prince Charlie known the enemies' numbers? Had he sent his army into battle on this dreaded moor knowing that the enemies vastly outnumbered the Jacobite forces?

Iain second-guessed his decision to leave the best of his warriors at the castle to safeguard his sister as he gazed over the bloody battle. Not all the bodies were warriors. Some were impoverished tenants forced to fight by their clan leaders with threats of imprisonment, death, or the burning of their homes, and some were hardly more than children.

He was thankful that at least his people were safe on the

island of Dorpol, but he would not leave the rest of his fellow Jacobites.

Murray, the commander of the right wing, shouted his war cry to rally his men. His brigade hollered in reply before running into the oncoming English army in a final attempt to hold them off. Other Jacobite warriors saw the charge and hurried to join, their war cries adding to the swell of shouts as men cascaded toward the English line.

With sword in hand, Iain rode his horse into the fray with the certainty that he would be killed this day. All the men alongside him had the same grim knowledge reflected in their eyes, but even so, the Highlanders surged into battle. Iain glanced to his far left. Why was the MacDonald Unit not moving forward? Had they not heard the command?

With no time for further thought, Iain charged. It felt as though he were possessed as he fought. All conscious thought disappeared from his mind as he focused only on surviving. At some point, the MacDonalds' battle cry sounding behind him pierced through his haze.

At the sound of their cry, adrenaline coursed through Iain, renewing his vigor. He continued to swipe at every English soldier he could until a cannon sounded so close to him, his horse reared, and having given the horse his head, Iain lost his loose grip on the reins and fell onto his back. Wind gushed from his lungs. A moment later, he was gasping for breath. Sweat dripped off his brows into his eyes, and with shaky hands, he wiped the wetness away.

His head spun as he fought to calm his breaths. He needed to stay alert, ignore the aches and pains from the many cuts and gashes covering his body, and choke down his fear if he wanted to keep fighting.

All Jacobite units were falling fast, and Cumberland's forces pressed their advantage until the Jacobites fled the field, fighting like madmen as they coursed through the lines of English forces to their freedom.

A voice shouted the command to run them down.

The Irish picquets moved across the moor, bravely intercepting the English so the Highlanders could flee the battlefield.

Iain, dazed and limping from his injured ankle, tried to follow his allies, but before he could make much progress, the government cavalry intercepted and herded the Highlanders south. He could just barely make out flags flying and pipes playing as government soldiers descended on them.

As he fought his way to the edge of the moor, he could no longer hear the screams or see anything other than his next quarry, his mind riveted on the fight and nothing else.

Abruptly, his sword found no more purchase, and he paused to look around. He stood alone in a muddy field of death. Shouts rose behind him, and he turned, prepared to fight anew, before slightly relaxing his stance. There were small pockets of fighting, but none were within a few hundred paces, and it was clear the battle was dwindling.

He wiped the sweat from his forehead but couldn't calm his frantic heart as he trudged after his countrymen still trying to escape the field, but a movement at the edge of the forest caught his attention. Sir Thomas, one of the enemy knights, had young Duncan to rights.

Iain sighed, remembering the season at Glasgow University when Thomas always picked on those weaker and smaller than himself.

Iain fought his way to where the men were standing.

Thomas glared at Iain and, kicking Duncan out of the way, raised his sword. "Laird MacLaren."

"Run, Duncan," Iain growled at the lad, but kept his eyes glued to his enemy.

Thomas laughed and waved his sword about. "I have dreamt of the day I finally kill you and your countrymen."

Iain's blood felt like ice as he took his chance, lunging at Thomas to try to strike him with his broadsword before he recovered his balance. The other soldier saw him at the last second and flung the flat of his sword against Iain's blade, blocking the blow.

The treacherous Scot cursed, "Jacobite horse dung, you can all go to hell." His cold gray eyes narrowed, and he launched at Iain, raining down a frenzy of blows in quick succession.

Iain blocked and jabbed, thrust and parried, but he couldn't find a break in the Redcoat's training. It had been wrong of Iain, wrong of all of them, to think they could match the enemy's skills.

Iain tried to draw in a much-needed breath, but his throat was dry, and his tongue was swollen. He had to make do with his painful pants, the air rasping in his throat. His arms ached, turned to slabs of great heavy stone, as his sword grew heavier by the second. The adrenaline he had felt earlier that day had fled him as quickly as his strength had, and he could sense his body was ready to give out.

Thomas parried Iain's half-hearted strike and pivoted, the point of his blade whistling through the air straight toward Iain's chest. Iain drew on every last bit of strength he possessed and raised his blade. Too weak to completely block its trajectory, he only managed to change its direction, and he felt the cold steel rip through his side.

He didn't know if the injury was serious; he couldn't feel the pain. He stared at the Englishman who came to Thomas's aid—the Sassenach, whose gleeful cry floated out over the field of slaughter. With one last effort, Iain raised his sword, knocking Thomas's weapon free, and brought his blade down on Thomas's head. Thomas ducked but not quickly enough, and Iain's blade cleanly sliced his ear from his head.

Thomas's howl attracted the attention of one of his men, and he hastened toward him. The Redcoat Sassenach clubbed Iain over the head, and he plunged face-first into the mud. An image of his sister filled his mind. Maeve was smiling at him with love-filled eyes.

Be strong. He sent the thought out to her, willing her to live a long and happy life.

A strange sense of well-being enveloped him. He knew he was going to die half-buried in the cold Moor, but that brought no fear. Instead, his heart ached for all the other dead, the young men who should still have had a lifetime to enjoy.

Darkness claimed him before he could say one final prayer.

ABBY'S HEART BEAT AGAINST HER RIBS SO VIGOROUSLY, SHE thought it would bounce out of her chest at any moment. Her eyes took in a strange vista, but her shattered mind could make no sense of it. Where was she? As if her hearing had caught up with the rest of her vision, a crack blasted through the stillness of the night. She jumped and screamed, but more blasts covered her shrill voice. She pressed her hand over her mouth; she had to stay in control of her fear. She couldn't be sure another scream wouldn't be heard.

Drizzly rain fell on Abby's head and on the open land before her. The lush marshland was objectively beautiful, but it sent a spike of dread through her nonetheless, and she shivered from the cold or shock—she wasn't sure which. Where was she? She should have been with her sisters and brother, warm and cozy, not freezing to death in the great outdoors of who only knew where. Her head ached, and burning tears fell from her eyes.

Abby squeezed her eyes shut as more blasts vibrated through her body. Guns. The blasts were from guns. Her eyes snapped open, and with her other hand over her heart, she twisted her head in all directions. Definitely gunfire, and there were a lot of them. Louder booms sounded. Her eyes widened, and she froze. Cannons? It sounded like cannons. Stifling another scream with her hand, she dove for cover, and an icy fist of fear tightened around her chest.

She silently thanked the lone pine tree now in front of her for giving her some cover as she huddled under low yellow-flowered shrubbery.

As her gaze flitted around her, she discovered she was on the edge of a battlefield. Realizing her breathing had become pants, she tried to slow her breaths.

She inhaled deeply and forced herself to exhale slowly, but her heart kept pounding against her ribcage and cold sweat beaded across her forehead. She peered through the foliage, frantically scanning the chaotic scene before her. Thankfully, she was some distance away from the battle, but as she watched men fall to the ground, a retch escaped her throat. It quickly blended with the cacophony of battle cries, gunshots, and clanging swords echoing across the field.

If there had been any doubt about her predicament, the screams and anguished cries coming from all directions made it perfectly clear that she had been thrust into a situation of life and death. She covered her face with her hands. "I want to go home."

She dragged her head up. Wishing wasn't going to get her home. The orb. That was the last thing she'd touched at home. She stared at her shaking hands. Where was the orb?

Careful not to make any sudden moves that might bring attention to her location, she bent her head, shook out the cloak, and patted down her clothes. Her heart picked up its pace as she felt the surrounding ground. She needed the orb to go back home.

More gunshots and cannon blasts out-roared an army of men's screams.

She looked over her shoulder through the back of her hiding spot to a couple trees and more low shrubs. She should go there to try to distance herself further from the battle, but the overwhelming noise had her rooted to the spot, and she stared once again at the battlefield.

Her every nerve trembled with fear. Her eyes bulged as more combatants became visible. Men in tartan were on foot and on horses. Scottish men, some holding long muskets, some with axes, scythes, or pitchforks, fighting mounted Redcoats. The English. She tried to think of places in the American Revolution that looked like her surroundings. She couldn't think of any, but that didn't mean there weren't any. She didn't want to believe it, but she was smack dab in the middle of a crazed battle during the American Revolution.

A bullet whizzed past her ear, breaking her stupor.

She pushed the cloak into her mouth to stifle a scream. She had to move as far away from the battle raging in front of her as she could. She pushed through the back of the shrub and crawled as fast as she could around and behind a bigger shrub.

Once she was behind the foliage, she kept her head down. The guns and their reports echoed in her head, and she jammed her hands into her armpits in a self-embrace. Now and then, a mortar would fire and have her heart nearly jumping out of her chest.

Blinking and trying to make sense of the sensory over-load, Abby wanted to scream, but she knew once she started, she wouldn't be able to stop. She had to keep control, think of what to do, but the only choices that came to her were fight or flight. She couldn't fight, and she was too scared to try flight.

The ongoing fire from the guns made her constantly jump, and the boom from the cannons shook the ground under her. The swords clashing and the chorus of screams sounded like a dreadful song. With every noise, her temples throbbed and her whole body shook. Keeping the cloak over her nose and mouth, she stretched out on her stomach, hoping no one could see her there.

Abby forced her brain to grasp for more information about the men, but she couldn't make out what they were yelling. Their shouts weren't in English. A loud crash of cannon fire had her snapping her head up. She hugged the damp ground and inched to the side of the brush just far enough to peer through the outer leaves. The contraption had no wheels. It wasn't a cannon; it was a mortar. Mortars had smaller ammunition than cannons, but to Abby, they were just as loud.

The details of what she was seeing made her heart flip.

To her right was what was left of one side of an army and a lone man still valiantly holding a flag. It was emblazoned with a thistle and St. Andrew's cross, with Latin script in a ribbon above. She murmured the rough translation without conscious thought. "No one provokes me with impunity." *Or something like that.* It was definitely a Jacobite flag.

Men in kilts, the English army, and a wet, bloody field. No, it was a moor. A moor in Scotland.

Battles of Scotland and England flitted through Abby's mind as she realized she wasn't in America anymore. She was in Scotland. She didn't know what battle it was, and she didn't care. All she wanted was to get as far away from the death and destruction as possible.

But without meaning to, her thoughts raced even faster at

the possibilities of her location. The names of the combat-ants filled her mind.

Charles Stuart, also known as Bonnie Prince Charlie, otherwise known as the Young Pretender, and he had wanted the throne of England.

She was certain she was right on the edge of the Battle of Culloden, but that would mean she had gone back in time. She wiped her hands hard down her face. Had she really time traveled, or was she asleep and all this was a dream? Or maybe she was in a coma. She couldn't remember having an accident, but she recalled the feeling when she touched the orb. That could have been her fainting.

Abby pinched her clammy cheeks. Surely it wasn't possible. Her parents' faces emerged in her mind. Had they really spent their lives traveling throughout time, collecting artifacts, and seeing history as it was being made? The orb. She scanned the area where she'd first arrived, hoping to see the slightest glint of the device in the few sunbeams that managed to hit the ground. Her chest tightened. Had she dropped the orb when she passed out?

No. Through the cacophony of horror around her, her logical mind surmised the orb had to have traveled with her. How else would her parents have returned home?

The ground was wet and muddy. Maybe she dropped it when she landed and fell on it. Maybe she pushed it into the mud. She had to go back and look for it. She had to get it.

More gunfire, mortar blasts, and screams broke through her thoughts, and shivering, she wrapped her arms around her chest. Whether the chills were from the cold or shock, she didn't know. A sob hitched in her throat.

She was really in the middle of the Battle of Culloden. The Jacobites' last stand against the English army, led by the Duke of Cumberland. And to make matters worse, judging by her surroundings, she was behind the already-defeated Jacobite line. As the English pressed forward, the Jacobites were being pushed to the upper edge of the moor. If they came further her way, someone would see her.

She cautiously squirrelled into the shrubbery.

Forcing her breathing to deepen and slow, she closed her eyes and concentrated on the sound of the air passing through her nose. That relaxed her somewhat, but the fighting continued to make her jump with its ferocity, and her body shuddered at each horrific sound. Silently, she willed herself to keep still.

She hissed out a breath. Part of her mind screamed none of what was happening was possible—there was no such thing as time travel—but the other part, the more logical side, calmly told her she had truly time traveled and was now on the sidelines of one of the most famous battles in history.

She had no choice. She couldn't go home without the orb, so she decided to wait the battle out and stay safe, and then she would get the time device and go back home.

Not more than an hour later, she watched as the English chased their enemy from the battlefield, and at long last, all was quiet except for a stray gun firing or a shout here and there.

She squinted out over the many prone bodies. Something moved. No, some*one*. One of the soldiers was still alive.

CHAPTER 4

Obscure noises infiltrated the calm blackness, and Iain tried to clear his brain of the pain radiating through his entire body. Pain? He smiled. Whether in his mind or physically, he didn't know and didn't much care at that moment—he felt pain, excruciating agony, but that made him happy. He must still be alive.

Instantly, another thought struck him. Was there pain after death? No. The pain was real, not something he perceived but a horror he felt in his flesh. He breathed in the stench of blood and death.

But it wasn't his death.

Iain pushed the pain out of his mind and listened with his ever-so-alive ears. Confusion filled his dim mind at the muffled noises floating around his still form. Sounds of battle so far away, he thought they might be a memory.

He forced his eyes open and compelled the fog from his mind. Where was he? A distant gun fired. All at once, he remembered, and he turned his throbbing head, pulling his side as he did so. He wrapped a hand over the site of new pain and felt sticky dampness covering his side. Examining his fingers, all he could see was black in the dim light. He lifted them to his nose and confirmed it was blood. He stilled. He was still alive, but not knowing how bad the wound was, he wasn't sure for how long.

He risked raising his aching head a touch to take in the battlefield. Too many bodies to count lay strewn over the moor. In the distance, more gunfire echoed, signaling that the battle wasn't over yet. Iain peered over the still bodies.

The English army fired at the backs of what was left of the fleeing Jacobite army, shadows in the lessening light, some falling, some outrunning the distance of the guns. He, apparently, had been left for dead.

Weary and feeling lost, Iain let the darkness take him under once more.

He woke again to the feeling of movement. Strange sounds carried to his ears. He opened his eyes and snapped them shut again at the sight above him. Brown hair falling about a beautiful face—a woman? She had her arms wedged in his armpits and was hauling him from the field, all the while grunting with the effort and, Iain was reasonably certain, cursing quietly. She looked down, and her wide blue-gray eyes immediately captured his gaze.

She stopped and dropped him. "Sorry," she said, sitting down beside his head, "but you startled me. Can you walk by yourself? I hope so, because you're too heavy for me to carry much further."

Furrowing his brow at her dialect, Iain looked around. Darkness had enveloped the moor, and he could hear no noise.

She nodded as if in understanding. "I think they've all gone. I got you off the field and under a shrub last night but had to leave you there because they came back and cleared the field of the dead and wounded. I snuck back tonight and

couldn't believe you were still there"—she glanced at him—
"and still breathing."

Thankful to be out of the enemy's clutches, even for a
small time, Iain cooed, "*Tapadh leibh, caile.*"

She sniffed. Drawing her cloak up, she wiped her face and
gazed at Iain with sad eyes.

He could only stare as if nothing else mattered at that
moment but to keep looking into those stormy blue eyes for
all time. Her gaze widened, and she turned her head.

"I don't understand," she whispered in English.

Her accent was unfamiliar. Perhaps she was from another
part of England Iain wasn't familiar with. He narrowed his
eyes at her. "Sassenach?"

"English? No . . . um, yes, I speak a kind of English."

He turned his mind to thinking in English. He'd learned it
well at Glasgow University but hadn't had many occasions to
use it since then. She said she wasn't English, but what did
she mean by "a kind of English"? Did she even know what she
was? Mayhap she had hit her head. "I will speak English, and
I said 'thank ye, lass.'"

She turned her gaze to his face, but he noted she didn't
make eye contact again. With a wry smile, she said, "I'm just
glad you're not dead."

He raised his eyebrows. His head throbbed, and with
every movement, dizziness threatened to overtake him, but
he saw the fear in her eyes. She was worried about him. He
wondered if he should have known her. Was she one of the
peasants he'd befriended in the last village he and his men
visited before the battle? Perhaps, but although he was probably the only one who wasn't completely drunk that night, he
still couldn't remember. He wondered idly if that night was
the last night he'd ever be happy again, before turning his
thoughts back to the matter at hand.

Regarding her once more, he decided he would have

remembered her no matter how drunk he was. She was a bonny lass. Even in the darkness, she shone above all other women he had met in his life, and he couldn't look away from her round, now blue-gray eyes dominating her smooth-skinned face. He only just stopped himself from reaching out and touching her sun-kissed skin.

Had he died? Was she his angel, the one to take him to the hereafter?

He tore his gaze from her face too quickly, his brain swirling around inside his skull. He pressed his hands over his temples and stared out over the dark moor. The lass had told him he wasn't dead.

Turning carefully so as not to stir his brain again, he said, "They are all gone, but they will be back again when it is light to make certain none were left behind."

She glanced at a lone tree between them and the battle-field, then stared at him with blank eyes. Pulling her cloak around her, she stood up and scanned the area as if she were deciding which way to go.

Was she thinking of leaving him there?

Iain gritted his teeth at the pain in his head and tried giving her his most charming smile. "I think the best course for us would be to return to yer village."

She shook her head, loose strands of brown hair swishing about her ears. "Village? Ah, no, that's the first place they'll look."

She took a step, and thinking she was indeed leaving, he pulled on her cloak. It snapped out of her hands and revealed the strangest attire Iain had ever seen. He gasped, his eyes popping at the tightness of her black trousers on her legs. Her white shirt was so thin, he was certain he could see her flesh through the flimsy material below her neck. The cut of her black coat was as a man's formal dress but shorter, much shorter.

Irritation washed over her face as she grappled with the sides of her cloak, replacing it over her body.

Iain had never seen the likes of her before. Her immoral clothes and her strange dialect had him backing up against the trunk of a tree. "Who . . . what are ye?"

"Never mind that now. Can you stand up?"

Iain couldn't move. He just sat staring at the angelic vision, wondering if he was delirious. Mayhap she was a faerie or a witch. Considering the way she was dressed, Iain's mind turned to a glaistig. She was beautiful enough to put a spell on any man. A shiver ran down Iain's back as he recalled that glaistigs, like all sirens, killed the men they enchanted.

Keeping as still as possible, he peered at her. The full moon's rays inching past the clouds proved her hair to be more red than brown, and he decided she had to be an angel. With stray tendrils loosely falling about her heart-shaped face, she couldn't possibly be anything else.

She turned to the left, and he could just make out the first curves of a braid.

He glared at her. "Nae human has such perfectly formed brows."

She looked at him, confusion springing into her eyes, but then she let out a short laugh. "Well, I do, buster." Those same brows drew together, and she mumbled, "At least for the time being."

Iain wondered at her speech. The way she said *buster* sounded like a curse.

She pulled on his good arm before he could ponder for too long. "At least try to get up yourself. I can't carry you."

"We should wait to make sure we are alone," he argued. "If there's anyone out there, they'll see us in a heartbeat if we try to move now."

She looked about again and sighed. "Fine."

The reluctant surrender in that one word told Iain that

she didn't like relinquishing control one bit. Witch or angel, he would learn soon enough. First, he needed her to help him stay alive.

They waited in the ever-growing silence until he was certain no one was about. He took a moment to study her as stealthily as he could. She appeared to be alone. But why would such a bonny lass be alone on Drumossie Moor?

"Why are ye oot here all alone?"

Her blue eyes sparkled as she thought for a moment before speaking. "I got lost."

"Why didnae ye stay hidden or run as far away from this place as ye could? Why did ye stay?"

"I didn't know where to go, and I was hiding, at least, until I saw you move." Her shoulders slumped as she sighed. "I couldn't very well leave you there. I didn't know how badly you were wounded, and once I had the thought that your enemy might come back and finish the job, I had to get you out."

"Ye could have been killed."

"Yeah, I thought about that while I was dragging you off the field. Anyway, should we go now?"

Taking her arm and forcing his leg muscles to cooperate, Iain managed to get to his feet. His head still filled with agony every time he moved it, but the pain in his side wasn't as bad as he would have expected. Mayhap the wound wasn't severe. He paused in his thoughts. Or mayhap it was so bad his body was masking the pain. He'd heard of people losing limbs and not feeling the injury until much later.

He gazed at the beautiful but scared angel. "There's a blackhouse not far from here. The Redcoats will have already searched it, as it lies in their wake."

CHAPTER 5

A blackhouse was a traditional type of cottage that often housed both families and animals, and Abby hoped he was right about the English having already searched all the houses in the area. "Good, that's where we'll go, then."

She didn't want to be anywhere near any of the man's enemies or their allies. What happened to the Jacobites after Culloden was one of the cruelest times in history. They were routed from their lands, hunted, and murdered. Cumberland, the leader of the English army, wasn't called *The Butcher* for nothing. If she was found with a Jacobite, she would also be killed.

She took a deep breath and tried to calm her body. She could freak out later when she was safely home. For now, she needed to get herself and her new companion to safety.

She glanced at him. Wariness mixed with curiosity filled his eyes, but something else sparked in the brown depths, sending a jolt of electricity through her chest.

The same thing had happened when their eyes met earlier

and, surprised at her body's reaction to just a look, she quickly gazed at the sky above.

Once away from his intense gaze, her breaths became normal as her own gaze found the moon and the dark clouds rolling over it. A second later, rain fell on her hood. Hard.

Sighing, she muttered, "Perfect."

She was tall, but with the man more than a head taller, she was able to duck under his good arm and help him limp further away from the empty moor.

Her one plan was to get as much distance between them and the battlefield as possible. If they were stopped and questioned, and if the injured man's reaction to her clothing was any indication, she would be in trouble. A lot of men of that time were barbarians and thought of women as their property. She didn't know what they'd think if they saw her clothes. One thing she did know was that they wouldn't listen to reason and they would think her mad if she told them the truth. They would probably just kill her.

The torrents of rain hindered her vision of a safe route.

Her nerves were strung so tightly that even the sound of their footsteps scared her, and although it was cold, she felt sweat drip down her back. Her eyes never stopped moving, peering in all directions, trying to discern any movement that might mean danger.

When had wolves become extinct in Scotland? She started and twisted her head to look behind for anything that moved. No. She tried to reassure herself. If that was the Battle of Culloden, then it must have been 1746, and she was sure wolves were gone by then, although, blast it, she remembered reading tales of them being around in the 1800s. She peered into the darkness. Great.

As quick as it had come, the deluge stopped. Moonlight slithered its way through the empty clouds, and Abby's heart bounded up into her throat. The light would show their whereabouts to anyone close enough to see.

She tried not to think of Englishmen finding them while she hustled the man as fast as she could through a small stand of trees. He gripped his side but kept up with her, and once on the other side, she exhaled in relief at the clear meadow.

She twisted her head to peer up at him. "How far?" she whispered.

"Cl-a-ose," he stammered.

Half-dazed with exhaustion and spent emotion, Abby let him guide them along their course.

And as they stepped on the green grasses, she gazed back. She still had to find the orb. She had to get home before anyone found her, before she was stuck in this hellhole.

Mashing her lips together, she hoped she could find her way back the next day. New fear swirled like a maelstrom in her chest. What if someone else discovered it first? What if it was buried in the mud and she lost it forever?

Stop it, Abby. No what-ifs. I will find it tomorrow, and it will take me right back home.

The man leaned on her more heavily and drew her back to the present . . . past . . . whatever. Logically, she knew she shouldn't be interfering. She could be upsetting the delicate history of time, and what of the consequences that might happen in the future?

She grimaced. There was a name for it . . . ah, the butterfly effect. Yes, a small change can make much larger changes happen.

Her meddling could be worse than killing a bug. He was much larger than a bug, so her saving him could be even more catastrophic than standing on a bug in the past.

Should she have just left him to die there? She scrunched her nose. No. She couldn't have done that, not once she knew he was alive. If she'd left him there, she would never have been able to forgive herself. She would have had nightmares of guilt forever.

He groaned.

Her shoulder ached, but she drove her back straighter, accepting more of his weight.

She listened to the quiet. No sounds of weapons, no thundering horses' hooves. Certain they were safe at last, her heart quieted.

Grunting with the effort, she pushed up harder into his armpit.

Why couldn't she have saved a smaller man? This one was gigantic. Even with his clothes between her palm and arm, she could feel the hardness of his muscles, the bunching and stretching of them as he lumbered beside her. Her thoughts became centered on the movement, the hardness, under her hand, and she fell into a rhythmical pace with the motion.

He let out a small groan, and her face filled with heat at her wayward thoughts. She'd never been so intrigued with a man's form before, and especially someone she didn't even know. Feeling foolish, she clutched a handful of material under his shoulder.

All thought of the man beside her evaporated moments later as pain coursed over her upper back. Grimacing, she worried they wouldn't make it up the incline, worried that if they didn't find respite soon, she would drop him.

Finally stepping on the crest, she spied a burnt-out building only steps away. Only half the gray stone facade was left standing, and almost the entire thatched roof was gone. Blackened stones were strewn over the ground, and the rest of the walls were crumbling slowly.

The smell of moist, scorched wood flooded her nostrils, but it wasn't nearly as bad as the stench they'd just left behind.

Thanks to the rain, the back section had been saved.

What was once an internal door had withstood the flames along its hem. Although it was blackened, the timber was still intact.

She sagged as she stepped to the door with a grunt. The man held on to a beam with the hand that wasn't clutching his wounded side and withdrew his weight off her shoulder. She sighed in relief at the loss of her burden and opened the door.

The room had been the middle of the dwelling, and thankfully there was a hearth built near the back wall. The peat was still smoldering. She loved how the Scots kept these fires going all year round. *Thank you, whoever you are*, she silently said to the owners of the house.

Another door to the side and behind the hearth stood open to the outside cold. Abby rushed to shut off the entrance as the man limped to the bed. He carefully lowered his body to the mattress until he stretched out on his back.

"Thank ye, lass," he said, and immediately closed his eyes.

Abby checked him. She didn't know if he was asleep or unconscious. Rubbing the freezing skin on her arms, she was glad either way—at least he was alive. He needed drying and warming, but she had to look after herself first or they would both die there.

Using a steel poker she found resting on the wall, Abby moved the peat about and then blew on it until small flares spouted out of the smoldering earth. She quickly added more peat and smiled at the growing flames. Thank goodness.

Looking around the modest room, her excitement at getting the fire working evaporated. She didn't think even a small family could live comfortably there, let alone with their animals. She shivered at the thought of living, no, existing like that.

The stone walls were crammed with a sort of earth mortar to keep the weather out and the heat in, but it was still cold.

The floor was dirt, but it was so packed, at first she thought it was concrete. Abby wondered how anyone could live on dirt. Above her, the wood beams held part of a thatched roof that she hoped was dense enough to block the rain, but not so thick that the smoke from the fire stayed in. She could already see where the soot had blackened the walls and rafters.

She placed more peat blocks on the fire and rested back on her heels, taking in the delicious warmth.

After her goose pimples faded, she removed her cloak and was surprised but delighted to find her clothes were only damp. She spread the cloak out in front of the flames.

Pulling a rickety wooden chair away from the corner, she sat facing the bed. Just a minute's rest and then . . . Uh-oh, she had to get him out of his wet clothing.

She studied his face. His eyebrows, as dark as his hair, weren't as bushy as she would have expected, although his eyelashes were much longer and darker than she had ever seen on a man. The growing stubble didn't hide his square jaw, strong but, at that moment, relaxed. His tanned and weathered skin told her he'd spent many hours outdoors. He must have led a physical life, because his entire body was taut and muscled. She knew he was big when she'd held him, but his shoulders nearly spanned the width of the bed.

The man groaned. Even with a pain-filled face, he was quite handsome. He probably had a family waiting for him somewhere, and she hoped she could make him well enough to go to them.

Standing up, she placed her hands on her hips, puffed out a breath, and went to work.

After pulling off his boots and thick socks, there was no choice but to rid him of all his clothes. They were soaked through, and mixing pneumonia with his injuries would just make her job all the harder.

Undoing the circular broach at his wounded shoulder, she pulled the long, wet plaid cloth from the front of his body, but it appeared to wind around his back. Something hard was amongst the folds. She carefully prodded and poked the cloth, revealing three knives. They were more like daggers than kitchen knives. She plucked them out and put them on the table.

Standing back, she glared at the deluge of material. How the blazes was she supposed to get him out of that? Maybe she could roll him off it.

She dragged the bed away from the wall so she could get around it, and then rolled him away. Holding him on his side, she pushed the material as far under him as she could. Once on the wall side of the bed, she nudged him to his other side and yanked the cloth out and off the bed.

Although she tried to be as gentle as possible, she knew from his moans every movement was hurting him. Performing the same ritual with his skirt, she finally rid him of his outer garments. His long linen shirt was next, and then he would be completely naked. She looked around for something she could cover him with, something she could drop there quickly.

Searching the room, she found a box under the bed. The leaves spread under and over the contents, Abby guessed, were to keep away bugs. At the sight of blankets, she called out in glee, "Thank the stars."

His shirt was long, and her arm muscles had turned to jelly from the previous exertion. There was no way she could repeat the maneuver. She couldn't pull the shirt up his heavy back, so she tore the material from the neck to the cuffs and then threw the blanket over him.

Now with less cloth to deal with, she forced her aching arms to drag and tug what cloth remained out from under his back. She grunted and swore until finally, with a little push against his shoulder, the last bit of linen broke free.

She felt bad for being thankful he was unconscious, but she was sure he would have been in excruciating pain with all the jostling and jerking otherwise.

After laying the plaid over the end of the bed to dry, she gazed at the ridiculous amount of material. From her recollection of history, the Jacobite army usually wore a long-belted plaid, but the tartan he bore wasn't as long, and she guessed it was his clan's colors, but she didn't know which one.

Moving to see how serious his wounds were, she hesitated. She should get out of her damp clothes as well or she would come down with a fever.

Removing her coat, shirt, and pants, she laid them out to completely dry. She was glad her lacy camisole had already dried from the heat of the fire, but she couldn't risk the man waking and seeing her in what to him would be scandalous and strange attire.

"There must be something in here," she said as she rummaged through the box. More blankets and men's clothes, trousers, tartans, and shirts, and then finally, a skirt and other women's clothing.

Keeping an eye on the man in case he awoke, she quickly pulled out a brown skirt and what looked like a sleeveless vest. They smelled stuffy, so she hung them from the rafters to air out. She would wear her shirt under the vest when it dried. The material was likely different from anything found in that time, but the cut was similar to a man's shirt.

She decided to sort through the rest of the stuff later; she had to tend to the man first. Eyeing him, she wondered what he was like. At least he wasn't awake, but even if he was, she would have plenty of time to escape before he came fully mobile if he was dangerous.

Abby realized she'd better see to his wounds before they

became infected. It would hurt—a lot. She silently pleaded to the heavens that he would stay unconscious. She spotted a bucket by the fire and groaned. Of course, there was no running water, but they had passed a stream close by. Great, there would be no bathroom, either, and having thought about water and streams, she needed to go badly.

By the time she had collected water from the river and poured it into a large cauldron over the fire to boil, she was hot and exhausted and ready for sleep.

How the people of that day dealt with what to her was the harshest of lives, she didn't know. She gazed up at the charred ceiling. "I want to go home."

CHAPTER 6

Finally, the water boiled, and she placed clean strips of his cotton shirt in the cauldron to sterilize the material.

Once she was satisfied they had boiled long enough, she wiped the tears aside, berated herself for being such a wimp, and set about cooling some of the strips of material in the freezing Scotland air.

Turning to the man, she took a sharp breath and began cleaning his wounds. He had many on his neck and chest, but most were surface scratches and cuts. The wound in the side that he'd held on to when he'd walked wasn't as bad as she had feared. It looked like a sword had just caught him. There was a cut, serious enough to worry about infection, but not deep enough to cause him any long-term discomfort. She wished she had some alcohol. At least then she could wash it better.

After laying a clean rag over the injury, she searched for more grievous wounds. She quickly checked his torso and down to his feet. Picking up his legs one at a time, she inspected the backs of his black curly-haired limbs. Nothing serious, only a few scrapes and superficial cuts.

She leaned forward and brushed his damp hair away from his high forehead. "I'm sorry, but I'm going to have to roll you over again. I need to see if there are any other injuries on your back."

With her arms still refusing to muscle up, she used her shoulder to manhandle him over as far as needed so she could examine his skin.

She sighed in relief when she couldn't find another wound and, as gently as possible, reset him on his back.

That only his upper body had met the swords and not one bullet had pierced his flesh was something of a miracle. She frowned. But why was he unconscious? Abby didn't think any of his injuries were bad enough for that.

Maybe he was just asleep. Fighting in war must have been exhausting.

Recalling Scottish history and the moor where she'd arrived, she was sure the battle had to be the Battle of Culloden and the Scot was a Jacobite. Although Jacobites weren't only Scottish fighters—some English sympathizers joined Charles Stuart's army. Irish Piquets, formed from regiments of the Irish Brigade and a squadron of Irish from the French army, also served in the battle.

However, his accent was definitely Scottish.

She gave a small shake of her head. The Jacobites were brave and fought to the death for their country and the Stuart king they wanted on the throne, but they didn't fare so well. She glanced at the door and wondered how long before daylight. She had to get back to her own time.

Another worry added to her previous ones.

The Highlanders were a superstitious race. What if they thought she was a witch? Would they burn her? Stone her?

He moaned, and his eyes fluttered open. He beamed. "God has sent me an angel."

Abby opened her mouth to tell him she was no angel but remembered the Scots' strong belief in God, and how some Highlanders mixed that faith with their long-held superstitions of fairies and other magic folks. She smiled back at him, noticing the specks of green in his warm brown irises. She could stare at those eyes forever, watching the jade flecks lighten and darken as if they pulsed to some silent inner rhythm. As he moved his head to the side, he grimaced and closed his lids.

❦

DEEP INTO THE NIGHT, ABBY WAS BECOMING INCREASINGLY anxious about staying there too long in case the English came back that way.

She wished the man would get better quickly. She had done her best with what was available, and she had kept his wounds clean and dressed. The scratches and cuts on his body were looking slightly healthier. They would heal, although some would leave scars.

What she was worried about was an infection. She sat on the rickety chair, watching him and dozing while he lay there like a baby and slept.

Sometime during the night, she had nodded off completely and fell to the floor. She awoke in a fright and remained confused until she realized where she was. Giving up her seat, she curled up on the floor in front of the waning fire.

Woeful moans floated to her ears. She willed her tired lids to open and blinked. She sat up and scooted away from the noise. Clearing the sleep from her mind, she focused on the form lying on a bed.

He flung his head from side to side and called out. *"Aingeal."*

Abby guessed he was speaking in Gaelic. Had he said angel? *I wish.* At least if she were an angel, she could fly herself right back to her time, to her family home, to her brother and sisters.

Rubbing her eyes, she returned to the bed and, as if in a sleep-induced trance, brought the chair close to him, sat down, and began wiping his warm face.

He kept ranting, sometimes in Gaelic, sometimes in archaic English, but always the word "angel" was interspersed in his ravings.

Drained and exhausted, she had somehow fallen asleep with her head on her folded arms on the bed. She opened her eyes, and they felt as if someone had poured sand into them.

The dawn heralded a bleak gray light into the room from the open windows, and she remembered where she was and with whom. She sat up and placed her hand on his forehead. It was warm but not feverish.

The dolt had tried to roll onto his injured side. His left leg was over his right, but his upper back was still against the bed and his face was contorted in pain. Abby pushed his leg alongside the other one.

She pressed him into the bed. "Don't move! Do you want to make it so this thing never heals?"

She hadn't meant to sound so harsh, but if she didn't manage his wound properly, the risk of infection was high. Abby just wanted, no, needed him to get well so she could leave and find the orb. Every moment there increased her chances of being discovered by the English, but she wasn't going to leave him, not until he could take care of himself. She would never be able to live with herself if she did.

During that first day, the sword injury began to look better. The surrounding redness had lessened, and it looked clean. He must have been an extremely fit man, because his body healed faster than she could have thought possible.

However, he was still weak from the blood loss, or some other hurt Abby hadn't found—she didn't know. He moaned, slept, and smiled at her at different times.

She would have liked to believe the smiles were really for her, but she figured he was probably delirious with pain.

Sometimes those smiles took in her whole being. Her heart fluttered when his intense gaze held hers for a moment and then traveled down the length of her body and back up to her eyes, where his smile often shifted to a twitch of humor, and she glared at him for laughing at her. But at other times, her heart nearly stopped beating at the menace that grew along his tight mouth and settled in the darkening green specks in his brown orbs.

She alternated between wondering if he was ogling her, chuckling at her, or if he meant to do her great harm. In the latter moments, she hoped he was delirious.

It didn't matter. For better or worse, he was in her care. However, if his look turned mean and she was certain he would live without her aid, she would leave before he had the strength to chase after her.

Her stomach rumbled, reminding her she hadn't eaten since Garrett's dinner. She took stock of what she had. Water. Maybe she could make a soup of sorts. She ventured outside and scoured the ground for something she could use. The heavy rain had ceased, but in its place, a persistent drizzle fell from the sky. She wondered if the sun ever came out in Scotland.

A noise she couldn't name sounded to her left. She halted and held her breath. Turning her head slowly in the direction of the sound, she started as a rabbit hopped into her line of sight.

It froze, and they stared at one another for a moment before the rabbit bounded off across the field.

Abby let out a laugh, thankful it was just an animal and not the English army.

Wild mushrooms grew in abundance, but uncertain which were poisonous, she decided not to pick them and went back into the cabin to search for anything they might eat.

After taking the damp vest off and laying it before the fire, Abby pulled everything out of the crate and collected another, smaller rolled-up blanket. She quickly unrolled it and found, to her delight, two loaves of stale but not moldy bread and a chunk of cheese. The owners must have been planning to come back for the box. Maybe they still would, and if they did, what would they make of her and the wounded man? She preferred not to find out.

Not wanting to linger there any longer, she wished he would wake up. She wanted to recover the orb, and he needed somewhere safer to stay.

Folding a cold wet cloth, Abby bent over to place it on his forehead.

He grabbed her hand and brought her fingers to his mouth, kissing them. "Thank ye."

Her breath hitched, and all she could do was stare at his lips, open enough to glimpse his surprisingly white teeth. His lips stretched into a smile, and she realized she was staring. She darted her gaze to his.

Those clear brown eyes were smiling at her. Was he laughing at her? She whipped her shaking hand away and sat back in the chair, gazing at the cloth in her hands.

He cleared his throat. "Water?"

That was a good sign. Abby jumped up and poured some cooled boiled water into a mug and held it to his lips. He drank thirstily.

"Not too fast." She moved the mug away. He reached out

for it again, his fingers brushing hers. Her heart picked up in tempo as her whole hand tingled at his brief touch. She put her reaction down to her excitement that he was awake at last. "Wait for a moment and then you can have more."

When she returned the cup to his lips, he clasped his hand gently over hers while he drank his fill.

"Thank ye. Who are ye?"

"No one. It's late. Go to sleep now and we'll talk in the morning."

And then I can find the orb and travel home.

CHAPTER 7

Her tone equaled one of authority. Iain didn't want to make her angry before he knew if she was human or faerie. His head ached, but after dozing on and off for what seemed like a long time, he felt well enough. However, his side throbbed, but he would have to look at it to know how badly Thomas had maimed him.

He recalled the battle and the final confrontation with Thomas. A smile twitched the corners of his mouth at the memory of slicing Thomas's ear. The *eejit* let his anger take over, and his wrath impaired his aim as his sword sliced Iain's side. He grimaced, but the cut wasn't sufficient to fell him. His head pounded at another recollection. Someone, not Thomas because he'd had him in his sights at the time, had clubbed him over the skull, hard. If they suspected he lived, the English would search for him, especially Thomas. Even with his injury, he hoped he was still strong enough to fight if he needed to.

He closed his eyes for less than a minute before slitting them open again and watching the lass.

The angel, or witch, Iain wasn't entirely sure, sat slumped

in the chair, her heavy lashed lids half-covering her view as if she were about to fall asleep. But every now and then, her lids lifted a little when she glanced to the door as if she expected someone to walk in at any moment. Mayhap she wasn't alone. Iain scoured his memory since he'd left the battlefield with her, but couldn't remember anyone else, no voices or sounds other than his and hers.

He took in her form. She had a strange beauty about her. He found it almost impossible to pin down what color her irises were. They kept changing from the deep blue of the ocean to a soft sky azure. With her alabaster skin, he knew without a doubt that she didn't work in the fields. His gaze locked on her lips, the hue of primrose petals and so plump, she appeared to be continually pouting. Would they taste as sweet as they looked?

He stared at her. The damp curly tendrils of dark red hair falling over her face made his fingers itch to push it back so he could see her more clearly. His gaze roamed down her braid she had brought over her shoulder, and his chest tightened.

She had disrobed and sat nearly naked, but she seemed so comfortable, as if she normally wore so little in front of a man. The snip of black lace bordering shiny material nowhere near covered her upper body.

She had bunched her skirt up, exposing long, shapely legs from the knee to her bare feet. Feet with perfectly pink-colored nails. His eyes snapped to her hands. How had he missed those nails?

Surely that was proof she must be a wood nymph. Only then would she have the power to harness the colors of the flowers.

Mayhap she wasn't even there. Had he succumbed to the fever? Was he imagining the nymph?

Or was she sent to take me to the afterworld? What an

exquisite guide. There was no way his imagination—and he judged he had a wonderful imagination—could have conjured up a beauty such as her.

Forcing his gaze away from her face, he noted her slender arms and smooth hands. She was no worker. But what sort of high-born lass dressed so immodestly?

He moved, and the shot of pain in his side reminded him none too politely of his injury. He groaned but ripped off the dressing and peered at the wound. It was superficial. The tenderness would go away with the healing.

She leapt up. "Keep still."

He ignored her and cautiously shifted his legs off the bed and sat up. He pushed the dull ache out of his mind by focusing on his predicament. If he was indeed dead, he would have gone to his maker.

She could not be an angel, this lass who spoke strangely. Mayhap from an English province he had not been acquainted with. She had to be Sassenach, which could only mean she was a spy. He flicked his gaze around the room. Why were they still in the croft? They should have already moved from the area. Was she waiting for someone? Cumberland, perchance?

He glared at her, and her eyes widened in surprise as she stepped backward.

"Who are ye?"

"Who are *you*?"

"I asked first, witch."

"I am not a witch, but if I was, you'd be a toad right now."

Iain pulled the blanket around him and got to his feet. A flash of dizziness washed over him, but he shook it away. Food and exercise would get his strength back. He had to return to his homelands. The English would be routing out all Jacobites and any who had aided them.

She stood straight-backed before him, wearing only that lacy piece and the skirt. Her eyes took on a stormy hue.

"Are ye a follower of the English?"

Her large eyes rounded; the storm within sparked lightning. "I am not a whore of the English, if that's what you're getting at."

Iain blinked at the mention of the word *whore*. He wondered at her ease with the term.

"Ye speak like naw other. Who are ye? Have ye come to take me to the afterworld?"

"You'll live." She rolled her beautiful eyes to the roof and threw her graceful arms in the air. "Oh, don't thank me. No, no, please, it was nothing."

Iain knew sarcasm when he heard it. He smiled at the way her eyes flashed with anger and her nose wrinkled with her words.

As she gazed up at him, her eyes quietened to a calm sky, but narrowed. "You should be thanking me, you know, not finding reasons to distrust me."

She smiled, showing perfect teeth. How could anyone have such perfect white teeth? Her whole face brightened with the movement.

His stomach knotted.

He didn't have time for dalliances. He had to get back to his people, to Maeve, his sister.

He straightened to his full height. The lass would be enough of a distraction even without a bloody war raging outside the door. But, those captivating eyes . . . She was too . . . no suitable word came to mind . . . *different*.

He frowned. What would Maeve make of the lass, he wondered as his narrowed gaze traveled down the length of her and back up to her face. "Who are ye?"

MAEVE STIFFENED AND NARROWED HER EYES AT FIONA, who had clasped a MacLaren server's wrist and pointed to her plate. "Take this away now. I have never tasted a worse bannock in my life."

Pink spots appeared on Leah's cheeks, and she took the plate away.

Maeve glanced at her friend sitting at the table closest to the dais. Jannet was once Maeve and Iain's nanny but was now a friend and confidant. She gave an almost imperceptible shake of her head, and Maeve looked down at her plate and tightened her lips.

If Fiona berated one more of the MacLarens' staff, Maeve would punch her in the face. She didn't care that the woman was supposed to be the next lady of the MacLaren clan, didn't care if she pushed the clan, Iain's clan, into war with the MacKinnons. All she cared about was how good it would feel to bloody Fiona's nose.

She silently apologized to her brother for her evil thoughts and wondered what Iain was doing at that moment. Was the battle over? Had it even begun? *Please be safe, brother of mine.*

Laird MacKinnon gulped the last of his ale and slammed the tankard down on the table. "More."

Maeve widened her eyes at Jannet. and she gave Maeve a slight nod, closing her eyes as she did so to indicate Maeve should acquiesce.

Maeve sighed and raised her finger to one of the serving staff. "More ale for the laird."

"And wine," Fiona said, holding up her goblet.

Maeve nodded to the server. "And wine."

Fiona gave the captain of MacKinnon's guard a smile. "And more ale for the captain."

He tipped his tankard to her in a salute.

Maeve frowned. If they kept drinking like that, they would empty the cellars.

"Why did MacLaren join the pretender's army? He knew we were coming here. He knew he was to marry Fiona. He should be here, welcoming his future family." MacKinnon pierced Maeve with his gaze.

"It was his duty."

"His army is still here."

"Iain would not take them. He wanted them here for my protection."

MacKinnon's face reddened. "Did he not trust the MacKinnons?"

"I'm sure he wasn't meaning ye would put me in danger. He was thinking aboot the English."

"The English have no quarrel with the people of Scotland —at least, those who don't join the battles raging all over the land. We who prefer to live in peace are not in any danger, lassie."

Maeve straightened her back at not being called "my lady." He was an obnoxious man, and she hoped with all her heart Iain would refuse Fiona. However, she shrugged. "I do not follow politics, Laird MacKinnon. I am the lady of MacLaren, and to that end, I am our clan's protector. If the English came here, I would offer our hospitality, but if they wanted a fight, I would offer one in return."

"Be careful what you say. There are spies all over Scotland, and the Jacobites are all but done for. Bonnie Prince Charles will be no more, and we must all protect our clans, our people, the people of Scotland."

"You have no argument from me, and as far as Iain is concerned, he wasn't pleased to be dragged into this war, but he is a man of honor, and he believes all Scotland's people should stand behind their prince."

MacKinnon snorted but stopped talking as he watched

one of his men stride into the great hall and stand before him. "A message, my lord."

MacKinnon read it and held up the piece of paper. "The Jacobites are finished. The English have won the battle and the war. We are now under England's rule." He picked up his tankard. "To England."

Everyone in the great hall stared at him and at one another, but none joined his toast.

His face turned bright red, and he stood up, pushing his chair back with such force, it fell with a crash. "Scotland is defeated. We can keep our holdings if we bow down to the English, but if we do not, we will be persecuted and stripped of our property. Now, raise your drinks. To England."

MacKinnon's men stood up. "To England."

Callum, a trusted MacLaren guard, bent and whispered something into Jannet's ear. She blinked slowly at Maeve and raised her glass. Maeve did the same, and once her clan followed, they all mumbled, "To England."

The captain of MacLaren's guard hurried down the aisle between the tables, followed by a thin, dirty young man Maeve recognized as Duncan.

"My lady, Duncan has news of our laird for ye."

Duncan bowed low. "My lady."

Maeve smiled, but her heart raced. Duncan looked grief-stricken. "What news do ye have?"

"First, I wanted to tell ye, Laird MacLaren saved me life. He was a brave man."

Jannet rushed to Maeve's side.

"Was? Are ye saying Iain is dead?" A large rock lodged in Maeve's stomach, but she searched her mind, her soul, and the connection between her and her brother was still solid. She stood up on shaky legs and gazed at Jannet, who wrapped her arm around Maeve's shoulders. "I don't believe it. He isn't dead. I would know if something happened to him." She speared Duncan with a quelling look. "Did ye see him fall? Did ye see his life leave him?"

"Nae. He told me to run and I did, but when I looked back, he lay motionless on the ground. The lowland traitor, an officer of the English army, was laughing as he and his men walked away from the laird."

Maeve's entire body shook. She fisted her hands. "Why dinnae ye go back? Why did ye leave him?"

"My lady, I tried, but the Scottish army had fled, and the English were hunting them down like boars. My only thought was to survive so that I may tell you the news."

"You did the right thing, Duncan," Donal said, and looked at Maeve. "I have been receiving news all this day. The battle was over before it began. The prince's army never stood a chance, my lady." He glanced down at his boots and back up and whispered, "Iain would want you to be strong in this. Ye must lead by example."

Jannet squeezed Maeve's sinking shoulders so hard that without her, Maeve would have fallen to the ground. Gathering all her inner resources, Maeve forced her shaky legs to keep her upright. She gazed around the great hall where her people sat or stood graven-faced, some weeping openly.

Fiona held her cup up to the captain of MacKinnon's guard as if in a toast before emptying it in one swallow. She tipped her cup at Leah, who was standing holding another plate of bannock. "More wine and ale."

Leah's tears rolled down her face unimpeded. She lifted her head, threw a knife-filled glare at the woman, and left the hall.

Maeve couldn't help smiling inwardly at that. She wasn't coming back.

Her heart told her Iain wasn't dead, and without proof, she refused to believe it. Eyeing Fiona, Maeve noted her gaze locked with the guard's. The woman was not to be trusted, and by all that was holy, when Iain came back, he would not be marrying her.

☙❧

ABBY NOTED THE CURIOSITY IN THE MAN'S EXPRESSION. He wouldn't swallow just any silly story even if she could come up with one. Although he was wounded—and wearing an old blanket—he stood before her in regal splendor. His eyes, dark as a moonless night, penetrated her soul. He would know the instant she lied.

She followed his gaze down her front. Darn. She should have put on her shirt and the vest, but she had been so busy and too tired to think about them . . . until now.

She plucked the shirt down from the rafter and quickly pulled it on, and stepping back, she slipped the white vest on, pinning it closed. She drew the skirt's drawstring round her waist as tight as she could. She didn't want it falling around her ankles anytime soon.

He'd been watching her the whole time with an expression she had no way of reading. "Who are you?"

He raised his brows. "I am Iain MacLaren, laird of the Dorpol MacLarens."

Great, Abby thought. *Why couldn't you be a nobody?*

She turned and collected the blanket of food, unfolded it, and broke off a piece of bread. She offered it to him. "Sit there and eat."

He took it but didn't put it into his mouth. "I want to know who ye are now."

"I'm, um . . . Abigail Davis."

"Abigail Davis. I dinnae know that name. Why were ye out on the moor?"

Abby didn't usually like being called by her full name, but the way he said Abigail, she figured she could get used to it.

"Abigaiel?"

"Ah, I came from America and was supposed to meet my grandmother, but I became lost."

"America is a far from here. How did ye get lost?"

Think, Abby. How did *you get lost?* She took a bit of bread and chewed as she tried to come up with a believable story.

"I had a seat in a coach, but when we stopped at an inn, I must have fallen asleep and the driver left without me. I walked the road the way we had been traveling, but when I heard shouting in the distance, I followed the sound, hoping to get help. I didn't know there was a battle raging and I got scared. So, I kept my head down and hoped I wouldn't be caught while I waited it out."

He sat down on the bed and took a bite of the bread, and then another, and soon stuffed the lot in his mouth. After washing it down with water, he held out his hand. "More, and some of that cheese."

"Please?"

He eyed Abby, and for a moment, she thought he was going to order her to give him the food, but he smirked. "Please."

Once he'd finished eating, he said, "Why did ye save me?"

"The English chased their enemy off the moor, but I stayed hidden in case they came back and during that time, I saw you move. Once I knew you were alive, I couldn't just leave you. That would have made me no better than a murderer." She shrugged. "I had no choice but to drag you off the field."

Iain frowned. "Others would have left me there."

"I'm not others."

"Naw, ye are not others." He said the words slowly, gazing intently at her.

The way he said that had Abby worried. Did he really

think she was some sort of witch? Once he regained his strength, what would he do?

She needed to change the subject. "You seem healthy enough now. Why were you unconscious for so long? Do you have another injury somewhere?"

"Naw." He rubbed the back of his head. "Being struck on the skull with something extremely heavy probably had a lot to do with it."

"Oh." Abby stood up and felt his head. "You have quite a lump there but whatever hit you, it didn't break the skin." She stepped away. "You were lucky."

"Aye." His eyes grazed over her. "I was very fortunate."

Standing up, he stomped his feet as if making sure his legs worked properly and flashed a smile. "And now it's time for me to take my leave."

CHAPTER 8

Did he say he was leaving? Abby blinked again, waiting for his words to penetrate her whirling brain. When they did, they sounded so final. He would just up and go? Just like that?

She scooped up his clothes, threw them at him, and spun away.

Facing the side door, she silently agreed with him. It wouldn't be safe to stay there any longer. The soldiers might return; they probably would. If she recalled the history books right, the English hunted the Jacobites mercilessly after Culloden. She frowned. Or brigands might be scouring the countryside for whatever remnants were left on the dead or alive.

"And where will you go?"

"I must go home."

He spoke quietly with warmth, and the sound of him handling the soft folds of material had her imagining him dressing.

She shook the image away and was thankful he couldn't see her guilty blush. "Where is that?"

"Dorpol. An island off the west coast. Ye cannae stay here alone, so ye will come with me."

An island meant it was a long way from where she had arrived. She couldn't go with him. She had to get the device.

When she never answered, he must have taken her silence as a no, because he said, "Ye must come with me at least until ye find yer grandmother. Where do they live?"

Uh-oh. Abby had never expected that question from him. She turned away and began folding the blankets on the bed. Think, Abby, what town is close to Culloden Moor? Inverness? It was quite a ways north, but she figured big enough to get lost in. She smiled. That sounded right.

She kept her back to him. "I . . . I think it was Inverness."

He took her arm and turned her around. He had dressed in his tartan skirt and pinned the leftover material over his right shoulder. It suited him. He would have been a movie star in modern times.

His jawline tightened. "We cannae go there. Cumberland's army will have taken hold of it by now. Ye saved my life and I am honor bound to keep you safe. Ye must come with me until we can send word to your family."

His tone sounded like he wished it were otherwise. Maybe he thought she would slow him down or do something stupid to give them away. But she was thankful she'd said the name of the town right, and more especially, that they couldn't stop there.

Heat filled her cheeks, and she hoped her relief at not being left in some medieval Scottish town on her own didn't show as she tried to make light of the situation. "Why, sir, I don't even know you."

His back straightened, and he placed his hand over his heart. "I told ye, I am Iain MacLaren, laird of Dorpol."

She snorted. "I'll just call you Iain, okay?"

The corners of his mouth twitched as if he tried not to laugh. "Iain 'tis."

Then he frowned. Scrutinizing her, his eyes darkened, revealing warmth, curiosity, decision. "We will travel as man and wife."

"What? Why?"

"An unmarried lass of yer looks would be fair game to any warrior or brigand."

Although Abby never saw herself as beautiful, she knew he was right, though she suspected a woman didn't need to be beautiful in this time and place, just available. She regarded his massive frame. No one would try accosting her with him by her side and anyway, the pretense only had to last until she got the orb to take her home. She nodded. "Fine, but we're only going to pretend, right? There'll be no sleeping together."

"It depends who we are acting for. We may have to share a room, but we have done that already."

"Fine, but when I said sleeping together, I meant no sex."

His jaw tightened and his lips thinned, and she thought he would argue, but he said, "I don't want to sleep with ye that way."

Abby wasn't sure if she should be offended at his statement, but she wasn't going to let him see that, so she grinned. "Shall we go, Husband?"

"Aye, *Wife*." He returned the knives Abby had found earlier into the folds of his tartan. "Collect what ye can and we will be on our way to Dorpol."

Still worrying over the lost device, she hoped with all her heart it would be easy to find, and then she would be on her way all right, on her way home. A frightening thought crossed her mind. *If the orb's not broken.*

No, she had faith in its strength. Even after her parents traveled so many years with it, it didn't have one dent.

Abby dismissed her misgivings and set about putting what clothes and blankets were left in the box in the largest blanket. At least with him, she would have protection.

She glared at Iain, who regarded her with near-unrestrained humor. "Are you just going to stand there and let me do all the work?"

"Ye are the woman, Wife."

She snarled. "Barbarian."

He laughed.

With him studying her so intently, she felt clumsy and unfocused. She picked up two small animal skins, probably deer, with thinner strips of skin hanging off them and turned them over in her hands.

"They be shoes."

"I know that." She sat on the bed and tied them onto her bare feet. They were a little small, and the straps cut into her flesh. They wouldn't keep her feet warm, but at least they might protect her soles from small stones and prickles.

She glanced at the muddy mid-heeled sandals she had arrived in. They would be even worse to wear. She picked them up and wrapped them with her modern clothes in a corner of the blanket. Better not let anyone in this time find them.

After wrapping up the blanket, she pushed it into his stomach. "You can carry it."

"As ye wish."

Abby walked out of the house with her head held high. She stopped and looked left and right. She wasn't sure, but she started walking in what she thought was the direction of the battlefield.

His chuckle followed her. "Not that way. We go south."

Without stopping, she said, "Not yet. I lost something very important, and I can't leave without it." *In more ways than one*, she thought.

"The English will be scouring the moor for survivors and burying the dead. We cannae go that way."

Abby spun around. "I'm not going anywhere without it, so if you want to go that way, you go. I'm not."

His mouth hardened in a straight line and his jaw twitched as he glared at her.

She blinked at his expression. He was stronger than her and could easily make her go with him, but she set her jaw and pierced him with a firm gaze. She had no choice; she had to get the orb.

After a moment of staring at one another, he said, "What is so important that ye would risk yer life?"

"It's an ornament and it's precious to me." She turned away. "That's all I want to say about it."

Gently turning her around, he gazed into her eyes. "I can see it is very important. We will go, but we will have to wait until nightfall."

She nodded, scared to say something that might change his mind.

He let go of her arm and made his way back into the cabin. By the time Abby joined him, he had a knife in each hand.

"We need food," he said matter-of-factly, and strode back out through the door.

Abby stood staring at the still-open door, hoping whatever he brought back was edible.

IAIN HAD AN EMPTY STOMACH AND IF THEY HAD TO STAY there until nightfall, he needed to try to find a rabbit or a pheasant to make a stew. He wasn't a stranger to throwing knives, but he wasn't as good as some, especially his sister, who always beat him in a throwing competition. He moved the knives around in his hands. *Mayhap with a hungry stomach, my aim will improve.*

He walked noiselessly through the heather and over the low bushes, wishing he had his dogs or at the very least, Donal and his hunting falcon. He crouched among some wind-stunted rowan trees and kept his eye on the mounds of grass tussocks close by. He held the knives ready to throw. He scanned the area for rabbits and after some minutes, he was rewarded with a ball of fluff scooting from one grass mound to another.

He threw the first knife, missing by a hair's breadth, but by the time he had the second knife up and ready to throw, the rabbit had bounded into the grass. He swore under his breath.

Mayhap the rabbit had family close by. He hurried to collect the knife and returned to his hideout and waited.

A memory stirred in his mind. The strange couple his father had befriended when Iain was six years old. They were from America and stayed with the MacLarens often during that year. Their speech was similar to Abigail's dialect; mayhap they had come from the same area. Iain, always a curious child, never discovered how they came and went. They didn't ride in on a coach or horses, nor had Iain ever seen them walk into the keep. They just were there, dressed in Scottish garb, and kept close to Iain's father. He never saw them leave either, and when he asked his father, he would joke and say the wood nymphs spirited them away.

Iain guessed their visits were secret, but when they left and never returned, Iain forgot about them as he grew older. He spent the next hour trying to remember their names.

The rabbit still hadn't ventured out of the grass, but another hopped toward the clump. He held his breath and threw the knife.

Picking it up, he said, "We have need of ye, my friend, and I thank ye."

On the way back to the blackhouse, he wrapped his tartan around his hands and carefully picked some nettles and then collected some mushrooms. Once he'd skinned and cleaned the rabbit, he pushed the door open.

Abigail turned startled eyes to him and then smiled. "Did you find anything?"

Iain held up the rabbit. "Ye can make a stew with half the rabbit, and the other half I will cut into strips to dry by the fire until we leave."

Abigail stood staring at him, so he pushed the rabbit forward. "Take it."

"No. I don't know how to make rabbit stew."

"Ye don't? Ye must be highborn to have servants do your cooking."

"I can cook, sort of, but I haven't cooked rabbit before."

Iain frowned. Rabbits were an abundant food source; how could she never have cooked the animal? He mumbled, "Mayhap I should have tried to get a deer."

Her eyes widened in surprise or fear, Iain didn't know, but she didn't say anything.

He deposited the nettles and mushrooms on the floor, moved to the fire, and added some more water to the cauldron.

"Make sure the nettles and mushrooms are clean, cut them into pieces, and put them into the pot. I'll look after the rabbit."

Iain began cutting up the rabbit as Abigail reached for the nettles.

"Stop!" Iain shouted. Abigail froze with her hand just above the pile of nettles. "Not with your bare hands. They are stinging nettles."

Abigail sat back. "Oh, of course."

Eyeing her, Iain had the strangest feeling she had never seen a stinging nettle before, let alone cooked with it, although she appeared to understand when he spoke. Had she eaten nettle soup before? He knew it was a popular dish in England, and he assumed it would be so in the Americas.

He kept silent, however, and added her actions to the list Iain was storing in his mind of the strange things Abigail did and said. He would find out the truth of her appearance on the moor and why she spoke differently from any other person Iain had met, be they Scottish, English, American, or French.

He would not risk the safety of his sister or his people by allowing her onto his lands. His only thoughts thus far were, was she a witch or worse, an English spy? If he could get word to her grandparents, he would learn the truth. Once he reunited her with her family, he could travel much more quickly to Dorpol alone.

When he was sure she was safe from the stings, he set about his work but watched her closely. He cut half the rabbit into chunks and put them into the pot. The other half he sliced into thin strips and hung above the fire along a length of chain he'd fitted there.

Soon, the aroma of rabbit stew filled the cabin and they both watched the pot. While waiting for the stew to finish cooking, Iain glanced at Abigail, who was looking at him with a curious expression. Their gazes met, and Iain, thrown by the blush that came to Abigail's cheeks, pulled his gaze from her and leaned forward and stirred the pot. It was either that or kiss the woman.

CHAPTER 9

Heat rose to Abby's cheeks each time her eyes met Iain's deep, dark orbs. He was as impressive as he was handsome, and she guessed his confidence came from being a laird of a large clan. Having people listen to him and follow his every order had to build character, and it was obvious he didn't lack self-assurance. Although she imagined some leaders grew power hungry, she suspected Iain was a considerate chief of his clan. He was, after all, cooking them a meal.

"It's ready," Iain said.

His voice filled the room and Abby gave a little start. "Good, I'm starving."

A frown creased Iain's forehead, and Abby wondered what she had said to make him irritable. It seemed to her every time she spoke, he became annoyed, angry, or exasperated. She couldn't quite tell which emotion his present expression showed.

The way he had looked at her when she'd reached to pick up the stinging nettles with bare hands nearly made her recoil in surprise. His furious eyes would have made someone less confident than her cower.

She glanced at him. Maybe he was just worried. If she'd touched the nettles, she would have been in pain for sure. She quickly looked away and hid a small smile. It was a stupid thing to do. She'd forgotten about the sting those plants would give, but only for a second. She suspected she would have caught herself before she actually touched them.

Her smile grew. If she wanted to keep him from changing his mind about going after her lost orb, she should just shut up. He was decidedly more relaxed when she kept quiet, so she accepted the bowl of stew and ate in silence as the darkness of a moonless night crept into the room.

Abby had to bite her tongue more than once during the meal. She had to be careful with what she said, and if she relaxed too much, who knew what would come out of her mouth? She took another mouthful of food. She had to admit she enjoyed the stew if she didn't think about what it contained too much. However, she hated the awkward silence. She always felt as if she should say something in those situations, but she was proud of herself for controlling that side of her and not speaking one word.

Iain ate his food without so much as a glance in her direction. He was obviously glad she'd kept quiet, and she got the distinct feeling if he didn't think he was in her debt for saving him, he wouldn't be taking her with him. She gazed at him through her lashes. No. He wouldn't have left her. He wasn't that type of man. Not like Peter, running away and leaving her to the muggers.

Thankfully, they soon finished with their meal.

Having already packed earlier, it took no time at all for Iain to collect the partly dried rabbit meat. Abby raised her brows as he tied the strips to his sword before he secured the blade in the scabbard on his back.

She guessed he saw her quizzical look, because he said, "The cold of the night will keep it from spoiling until I can finish drying it in the sun tomorrow."

Abby wondered again if the sun ever came out in Scotland but kept her thoughts to herself and nodded.

He held out his hand and she stared at it. "Take it," he said.

Her fingers trembled at the thought of placing her hand in his rough, massive one. She made a fist. "That's okay, I'll just follow you."

"It's dark and I don't want us to be separated." He waggled his fingers. "Take it." When she didn't immediately do so, he said, "We're nae going anywhere until ye do."

She shrugged and held her breath as she placed her hand in his. She was right; her fingers tingled, and a jolt of electricity speared up her arm. Watching her with his piercing gaze, he tightened his clasp, which only accentuated the effect. Not knowing what else to do, she nodded, letting him know she was ready to go.

All the way back to the moor, Abby prayed the orb was still there. *Please be there. Please be there.* It kept her mind off the weird feeling her hand in Iain's elicited within her. If she stopped concentrating on the device for more than a few seconds, her fingers prickled at the warm glow that spread through her body. His skin wasn't rough exactly, but thick, like tanned hide. She sensed the strength in his hand and was thankful for his company in the cold night.

She had pulled her skirt over her other hand to keep her fingers out of the cold air and hastened her steps to keep up with his massive strides. They kept quiet as they approached the windblown trees they had hidden under just three days before.

Iain pulled her hand down as he stooped low, and then withdrew his hand from hers. Abby bent over, trying to make herself as small as she could, although she doubted anyone would see them. The night was darker than she'd ever experienced. She looked up at the sky. Not one star, let alone the moon. She shivered, surprised at just how cold it had become without his hand holding hers.

He knelt behind a clump of grass and tugged her skirt to indicate she should do the same. She did and pointed to the lone tree ahead of them. "I think I dropped it around there," she whispered close to his ear.

As she spoke, the clouds parted ways and the moon's light shone over the field. Abby ducked lower. Large shadows of people moved about, and two men in uniform walked toward her and Iain. Abby held her breath. They were going to get caught.

Iain placed his hand on her shoulder as if for reassurance. The soldiers stopped, and one bent down and picked something up, something from near the tree where Abby first arrived on that dreaded moor. It glinted in the moonlight and Abby gasped. She clapped her hand over her mouth before the sound fully escaped, but Iain pushed her down into the earth. She had to use both hands to stop her face from being buried. She wriggled around and tried to stop him from crushing her further.

His hot breath made the little hairs around her ears stand on end. "Stay there," he growled deep and low in his throat.

Her eyes narrowed, but she did as she was told.

A man shouted, "Sir."

"What is it?" another man answered.

"We found something."

"What?"

Boots sloshed in the still-wet ground, but Abby couldn't tell if they were coming or going.

Iain's hand moved from her back and Abby lifted her head

to peer over the bush. Her hand covered her mouth before she let out a sound.

"What have they got?" she whispered to Iain as the two men walked back to the group of soldiers. A tall, thin soldier met them before they joined the group and took whatever it was from one of the men.

"I don't know, but it is white and shiny."

Abby didn't have to see it to know it was her orb, her time device, her only way home. The soldiers spoke, but Abby couldn't make out what they said. As the tall soldier turned away, the orb shone proudly in the moon's light. Abby's heart sank as her one and only way of getting home was taken away from her.

She couldn't let that happen. She had already worked out that when she turned the orb, so the gold leaves became whole, it took her back in time. All she had to do was tackle the soldier and take the orb, twist it to break the leaves' connections, and she would return to her own time. She was sure it would happen too quickly for anyone to hurt her.

She moved to get up, but Iain's hand pressed down on her back, pushing her into the dirt.

She quickly turned her face so only the side of her head was buried. "I have to get it back. Please let me go," she pleaded.

"Don't be an *eejit*. That man with the ornament is Sir Thomas, one of the duke of Cumberland's knights. He will not care that ye are a lass. He will kill ye."

Abby's shoulders slumped, and she stopped fighting. *Butcher Cumberland*, that was what the duke would be called in history books. If the man who had her device was one of his knights, then he, too, was a sadistic butcher working to rid the land of Scotland of all his enemies.

Iain must have noticed her give in, because he took his hand off her again. She sat up and wiped the side of her face, first with her hand and then with part of the skirt she hoped wasn't also sodden with mud.

The one Iain called Thomas mounted his horse and called the men to follow him. Some on horses and the rest walking, they headed toward the other end of the moor.

"I need it," Abby said, nearly choking on a lump in her throat. She didn't even try to stop the hot tears falling down her cheeks. She was never going to see home, never going to see Garrett, Max, Izzy, or Bree again.

She dropped her head into her fabric-covered hands and sobbed her heart out.

After a minute, Iain scooped her up into his arms and held her close to his chest. "Shh, lass. All will be well."

He stroked her head, trailing his fingers along her braid. "All will be well."

In another time and place, Abby would have enjoyed his ministrations, his every touch, his voice. His strong arms comforted her, and his voice was so gentle, she almost believed that all would be well, but she had to be realistic. She was stuck in eighteenth-century Scotland.

Abby wept quietly at the loss of her family.

"I will get it back for ye," Iain soothed.

She sniffled noisily but kept her head pressed to his chest, strangely drawn to the beat of his heart, loud and strong, in her ear.

Iain patted her on her back, and Abby pushed away. She couldn't get too comfortable in the man's arms. She had to keep her distance. There was no way she could get close to an eighteenth-century Scotsman. The very idea was just too ludicrous.

But did she hear him right? She wiped her wet face on her skirt and looked up at him, almost afraid to ask. She sniffed. "Did you say you would get my, um . . . treasure back?"

SIR THOMAS AND A SMALL REGIMENT SCOURED THE MOOR for the Laird MacLaren. "I saw him fall." He rounded on his man. "You didn't kill him. He has survived."

"I was certain he was dead, my lord. Someone must have taken his body or, if he was alive, helped him from the field."

Thomas glared at the ground as if it had swallowed MacLaren to stop him from finding him. "You were always a step ahead, but in this, you will not evade me, MacLaren."

A soldier called out, "Sir."

"What is it?"

"We found something."

Thomas's pulse warmed at the thought it was Iain. He had to be certain the man was dead once and for all. He sloshed through the mud. "What?"

The soldier handed Thomas a white trinket. He turned it around in his hand. "Mayhap this belongs to MacLaren. Mayhap I will return it to his sister."

He smiled at the thought of Maeve thanking him for the trinket. She was a beauty, and he oft thought about her on cold lonely nights.

Thomas pushed the egg into his coat and mounted his horse. A messenger galloped onto the other side of the moor.

"Follow!" he ordered his men.

His men, some on foot, some on horseback, followed Thomas to the approaching messenger.

Pulling his horse up alongside Thomas's mount, the messenger handed him a missive. "From Lord Cumberland, my lord."

Thomas read the letter. He and his troops were to go to Aberdeen immediately. He turned and gazed at the place where MacLaren fell. *Aberdeen can wait until I have found MacLaren dead or have killed him for certainty.*

He gave the messenger a sharp nod of his head, and understanding, the man galloped back the way he had come. Thomas scrunched up the missive and poked it into his pocket along with the stone egg. He turned his horse north. "We ride to Inverell."

☙❧

IAIN GAZED INTO ABIGAIL'S BLUE EYES, SO CLEAR NOW THAT they were free of tears, but also so hopeful. He didn't want to disappoint her, but her treasure was just a thing. His family was his life and he needed to make sure they were safe.

"Aye, I'll find your trinket, but not this night. Once we get to Dorpol, I will send word out to find yer grandparents, and then I will take my men and find Thomas and yer treasure."

She lowered her head. Iain hoped she wasn't going to cry again. He could put up with anything, pain, loss, even someone shouting at him, but he never knew what to do when a woman cried.

One thing he didn't want was to hold her again. He had done so without thinking earlier, and the pleasure he felt at her warm breath touching the exposed skin below his neck had him pulling her closer. As soon as she was out of his arms, they felt empty, and the sense of loss confused him.

No, he couldn't risk becoming involved with the likes of her. Not when he was all but promised to another woman. Fiona was Scottish and having the MacKinnons as allies would strengthen his clan.

His gaze took in Abigail. The lass was too different. He tilted his head. Too mysterious.

A gunshot sounded in the distance, and a shout rang out over the moor. Iain recognized Thomas's voice and snapped his head up. A regiment of English soldiers, Thomas in the lead, raced toward him and Abigail. He threw himself on her, grimacing at the sound of her face being buried once more in the moor soil.

Her cry was thankfully muffled.

"Shh," Iain whispered into her ear.

The horses galloped past them, and Iain let out a breath of relief. They weren't after him and the lass. He waited until the foot soldiers ran past before he let Abigail up.

"I'm sorry, but if they caught us—"

"I know, I know, they'd kill us."

"Aye."

This time, Iain unbuckled his tartan and handed the copious material to her.

She wiped at her face and glared at him. "Do you have to keep pushing me into that stagnant, putrid mud?"

"I had to hide ye."

"You could have done that without half suffocating me." She pulled more of the material to her and kept wiping. "I need a shower."

Iain gave her a quizzical look and tipped his head back to look at the sky. The clouds were nearly all gone. "I don't think it will rain, although I see why ye would want it to."

Her eyes narrowed at him as he flicked a spot of dirt off her cheek. Her mouth formed an O, and his heart missed a beat at the thought of kissing those luscious lips.

He sat up, gazing in the direction the English had gone. Abigail tugged at the tartan to continue wiping away what mud she could.

An orange-yellow light rose above the trees and Iain growled. Thomas had found the blackhouse and set fire to what remained of it after the last blaze. He hoped he and Abigail hadn't left any tracks that would lead them back to the moor. He jumped up.

"Quick," he said, holding out a hand to Abigail.

She looked at him questioningly.

He nodded to the fire and she looked in that direction. She gasped and took his hand, letting him pull her up.

They gathered their belongings and Iain guided her east, away from the moor and away from Thomas and his men. He hoped he could find horses to get them to the nearest port.

CHAPTER 10

Iain and Abigail walked all night except for an hour when they found another burnt-out shell of what was once a home and rested. By the time the gray light of dawn filled the sky, Iain was tired, but he was used to all-night hunting trips. However, the lass was exhausted and stumbled more often than she trod behind him.

"Are ye all right?" he asked for the hundredth time.

"No, my legs are numb." She stopped and fell to the ground.

"Wait there. I'll go atop the rise and search for somewhere safe to sleep."

She didn't answer, just laid her head on her crooked arm and, he guessed, fell asleep.

At the bottom of the hill, Iain glanced back. Abigail was a lump of brown on the brown grassy field. With her not moving, she looked like a clump of dead grass from a distance.

Voices rose up in the air behind the hill. Iain fell to his stomach and shimmied up the crest until he saw over the rise. Horses and a cart slowly rolled down the road.

Iain immediately recognized the MacDonald colors in the men's kilts and the women's shawls. The MacLarens and the MacDonalds had never been friendly, and while the last battle they'd fought raged in the fifteenth century, they would never become allies.

Iain squirmed down the hill and once he figured he was out of sight, he stood up and ran back to Abigail.

"Quickly, get up," he said as he pulled on her arm to make her stand.

She groaned and tried to roll over. He placed his arms around her waist and yanked her up onto her feet.

"Wake up, lass."

She stood there swaying in his arms, her eyes still shut. He shook her. "Wake up!"

Her eyes snapped open, though she stared as if not seeing. He gave her another shake. "Wake up."

Recognition slowly came to her eyes. "Stop shaking me. I'm awake." She brushed his hands off her. "What?"

"Hurry." He grabbed her hand and pulled her along behind him, hoping the MacDonalds had not moved past.

She yanked her hand away. "I can walk myself."

Iain shrugged and kept going.

"Where are we going, anyway?"

They were at the hill. "Be quiet and keep down."

He dropped onto his hands and knees, and crawling up the rise, he turned to her and gave her an expression that said to do the same. She looked down at her mud-encrusted skirt, shook her head, and, bending low, followed him.

Once at the top, Iain fell onto his stomach again and waved her down. She flattened her body out beside him.

As the horses and wagon passed by, he swore in Gaelic. Surely these men fought side by side with him on the moor? With closer inspection, Iain dismissed that idea. These people were landsmen, not warriors.

Hoping he was doing the right thing, he stood up, ran to the road, and called out, "Stop."

Three men turned their horses around and stopped. A small lad, a young man, and an older man. They might welcome another sword.

One with a wild blond mane said coldly, "Why might a MacLaren waylay us?"

Iain's hopes fell. Some MacDonalds still harbored ill-will toward the MacLarens.

A curly brown-haired man moved his horse forward a step. His face was lined with age, but he held himself with strength. "Whit are ye doing here, MacLaren? Have ye misplaced yer clan?"

The fair-haired man laughed.

Iain ignored him and held the older man's gaze. He indicated Abigail should move to his side. She did, and putting his arm around her shoulders, he pulled her close into his uninjured side. "This is ma wife. Our croft was burned, and we need help to reach the coast."

The older man raised his brows. "The English are scouring all of Scotland for Jacobites. Might ye be one?"

Iain didn't want to lie, but he had no way of knowing if the men were English loyalists. Although the Jacobite MacDonalds were on the battlefield fighting beside him and the other Jacobites, Iain wasn't certain that all members of that clan thought the same. "Nay, we lost everything in the fire and need to return to family."

The three men exchanged looks, and the older man leaned forward slightly. "We have naught to offer."

Iain well understood. His presence would put the man's family in peril.

He slightly bowed his head and was about to turn Abigail away, but a woman called out, "Wait."

A full-bodied woman jumped off a cart and hurried to the

man. Her dark hair blew over her face, and she shook her head to clear the strands from her eyes. She caught her hair up in a strip of material and tied it at her nape. "We have enough, Colin." She smiled at Abigail. "Whit be ye names?"

Abigail opened her mouth to speak, and Iain hurriedly cut her off. If these people heard her strange accent, they might not help them. Mayhap after they learned they could trust them, they would be more open to her. "I be Iain MacLaren, and this be Abigail." He glanced at the lass and added, "Ma wife."

"I'm Mary, and that be my husband, Colin." She waved her hand behind her. "These are our sons; the blond rebel is Parlin, and the lad is Tavis."

She gazed at Abigail with concern filling her eyes. "Ye look worn out, lassie." She raised her hand to touch Abigail's hair, but drew it back and looked her up and down. "You be the dirtiest lass I have ever seen. Colin, we need to stop at the burn."

Colin huffed. "Muire."

The woman gave him a glower that said *ye won't be arguing with me*, and Iain had to stop himself from smiling.

Colin must have known that stare well, because he sat back and nodded once.

Relieved, Iain eyed the horses, wishing he could ride. His glance swept over the already laden cart. It appeared sturdy enough to carry both his and Abigail's weight. Following Iain's gaze, Colin said, "Tavis, let Iain have ye horse and ye can ride in the cart. I'd like to talk to him some."

Thankful for the man's change of heart but wary about what he wanted to discuss, Iain nodded. "Thank ye."

Abigail said, "Iain was injured in the fire at the cabin. He cannot ride a horse."

Iain gently nudged her toward Mary. "I am well enough, Wife."

83

He glowered at her, hoping to quiet the woman. Her strange way of talking would only have the people asking questions, questions he had no answers for.

She narrowed her eyes at him and shrugged. "It's your life."

The woman, Mary, or Muire, her Gaelic name, regarded Abigail with curiosity. Iain tensed but breathed out in relief when she didn't say anything. Instead, she helped the lass onto the wagon.

Mounting Tavis's horse, Iain bit back the shooting pain in his side. He didn't want Colin to change his mind about letting him ride a horse. He needed the mount in case the MacDonalds were traitors and he needed to whisk Abigail out of their clutches. Many Scots aligned themselves with the English.

And while Iain fought alongside the MacDonald clan only days before, he wasn't certain that every MacDonald was loyal to Scotland. He decided they had yet to prove themselves trustworthy.

Once settled in the saddle, Iain took the reins and rode alongside the cart Abigail settled on. He shot her a hard glance, hoping she would keep her chatter short, but he needn't have worried. Abigail answered Mary's questions with good grace, saying she was from the Americas and had met Iain when she came to Scotland to visit her grandfather.

Mary appeared to believe her.

The continuous ache in his side had Iain worrying for his life. He'd experienced fevers in his younger days, and he knew when one was growing inside him. He wanted to get to Dorpol before it overtook him completely.

His sister was adept at healing and would aid him back to health. He sighed at the thought of Maeve. He had left his lands in her care for too long, and it was time he returned and took on his responsibility as laird.

He absentmindedly held his side. If they didn't get to Dorpol in time, Maeve would be burying him instead of tending him. His gaze shifted to Abigail. He wanted to get to know her better, but he would have to live for that to come to pass.

As the day continued, Iain constantly found himself staring at the strange woman, his angel. With the very mortal feelings she imbued in him, he wondered if she'd put a spell on him. He had never been as attracted to, as curious about, or as confused by a woman before. While he liked to think of her as an angel, for she looked like one, he knew in his heart of hearts she was as human as he was.

But could he really believe she was a stranded innocent? He didn't want to consider the alternative. He had a feeling she was hiding something, but somehow, he didn't think it had anything to do with the war between Scotland and England. And she didn't appear to be masquerading as someone else. Even though she acted strangely to his way of thinking, her actions were natural. He gazed at her dirty but open face and frowned. He'd been to France, and not even in Louis's palaces had women like her existed.

He eyed her figure. She sat with her back straight, but by the slope of her shoulders, she wasn't tense.

Even in peasant clothes, she would shine in a group of women of gentry. She moved to the side of the wagon, pulled her knees up, and rested her chin on them, gazing at Iain. His breath hitched at the admiration in her eyes.

He looked away. Those stormy eyes penetrated his very essence. He still couldn't decide what color they were. Blue or gray? They were neither, yet both.

Her laughter brought his eyes back in her direction. He wished he'd made her laugh that tinkling melody.

He raked his eyes over her. She gazed up at him, something akin to fear reflected deep in her eyes, along with something else . . . want? The emotion reaching out to him snatched his breath away. Her orbs once again stormed, swirling eddies pulling him under. He forced his gaze away and focused on the road ahead. He near drowned in those eyes.

"MacLaren," Colin called to him, and signaled Iain to ride alongside him.

Iain kicked his horse into a trot and brought it back to a walk beside Colin.

"I know ye are a Jacobite, MacLaren."

Iain opened his mouth to deny the charge.

"No, dinnae try to lie to me. I'm not an *eejit*, but dinnae worry, we are MacDonalds, and even though I would not follow the pretender, I would never be disloyal to Scotland."

"I'm glad to hear that. Many MacDonalds lost their lives during the battle, and I am proud to have fought alongside them."

"Aye, my brothers fought, and I was hoping to come across them on the way to Inverness. I have heard Bonnie Prince Charlie has sent orders through the ranks for everybody to shift for himself as best he could. Is that what ye are doing?"

"I hadn't heard that order, but aye, that is what I'm doing."

"Is the lass really ye wife?"

Even though Iain felt comfortable talking to Colin, he managed to keep to his lie. "Aye, I made it to her parents' home, and now we must get to Dorpol."

After a few miles, Iain fell back to ride alongside the cart. He chanced another glance in Abigail's direction. She had curled up in the corner of the wagon with her eyes closed. She seemed to be sleeping. But, as if she sensed his gaze resting upon her, her sleepy lids slid open, and once again, her gaze penetrated to his soul.

He had sagged in his saddle and tried to straighten his back, but the movement made him groan in agony. He couldn't swallow the sound quick enough and knew she had heard him when she asked Mary, "Are we going to stop soon?"

Just then, Colin shouted over his shoulder, "We will camp here this night."

He veered his horse off the road and into a clearing.

The cart followed him. Colin and Parlin unsaddled their horses and hobbled them before unharnessing the cart horses. They, too, were hobbled and led to a stream.

The women filled buckets from the stream, and as Iain tended his mount, Tavis ran up and said, "I'll look after Donny."

Iain patted the horse's neck. "Thank ye for being such a grand mount, Donny."

Tavis grinned as if he had been the recipient of the compliment and set about unsaddling and rubbing the horse down.

With nothing to do for the moment, Iain watched Abigail talk and laugh with the other women at the water's edge. Mary and the other younger woman washed Abigail's hair with buckets of water from the stream.

The lass must have said something funny, because Mary hit her playfully, and they both fell about laughing.

Once they'd caught their breaths, they both glanced at Iain. Mary's eyes were full of merriment, but Abigail's were filled with swirling clouds of . . . sadness?

Iain drew his brows together. Was she mad? Laughing one minute and near crying the next? He shook his head. He'd never understood the complexities of a woman's emotions.

As he helped build a fire, Iain realized he felt no pain. He wondered if that was a good or bad thing, but he decided to enjoy the relief while it lasted and collected as much firewood as he could handle to thank the MacDonalds for their kindness. All the while, his gaze kept wandering in Abigail's direction as she dangled her legs in the cold water and washed as much of herself as possible.

By sunset, the pots were boiling, and the aroma of the dried beef stew had Iain's stomach reminding him neither he nor Abigail had eaten all day.

She sat on a blanket and accepted a bowl from Mary with what Iain recognized as a tentative smile. She squinted into the bowl, her face telling him she wasn't sure what she would see in there. The trepidation in her eyes made him wonder if she expected whatever was in the bowl to jump out at her at any moment.

He drank from his bowl with an eager slurp, let out a moan of contentment, and nodded to her. "'Tis very good."

After another slight grimace, she breathed in the aroma before delicately sipping. She shot him a wide smile and seemed to enjoy the rest of the bowl's contents.

"Iain," Mary said, handing a piece of bread to him. "My mother would like you to try her bread."

Iain smiled at Mary. "Thank ye, but please, what is your mother's name?"

An older woman slid beside Mary. "I am Fenella."

Iain took a bite of the bread. "It is very good bread, Fenella. Thank ye."

Fenella gave some to Abigail and called to the child. "Blair, leave the horses alone and come and eat."

The child gave one of the horses a handful of grass, and answered, "Yes, Nanna."

Once they'd eaten and the camp readied to settle in for the night, Abigail gazed into the fire, appearing to be lost in thought.

Iain plonked down beside her with a grunt. "Sleep, Wife."

She jumped, startled. "Don't sneak up on me like that."

He raised an eyebrow. With his injury, he could not sit

down without making a sound. "What were ye thinking aboot?"

"Home."

He regarded her profile. The light from the fire cast orange hues over her skin. Shapely brow, a downcast eye, delicate but straight nose, lips so full, they seemed constantly ready to be kissed. He pulled another blanket over his back and hers. She turned to him, her expression one of confusion.

He bent close to her ear. "We are man and wife to these people. Would it not look strange if we didnae share a bed?"

She stiffened and stared at him, the fire's light catching her hair so that the red in it blazed as hot as the flames. The light flicking on her flawless skin cast an ethereal glow about her.

How he would love to push his face into that hair, graze his lips along her bonny dimpled chin, to smell her, taste her. And once again, guilt filled him. He had to stop thinking along those lines. He was to be married.

"Good grief," she murmured with a shake of her beautiful head. "Fine, but keep your distance."

Iain grinned. "Tell me more of yer homeland. Is there no one who has yer heart?"

"Not that it's any of your business, but no. There's no one. But that doesn't mean I'm available. I'm pretty choosy about my sleeping partners."

Why a shot of joy ran through him at her confession, he didn't know, because her face screamed sadness at the admission. He frowned. She had said her sleeping *partners*. Had she had men in her blankets before?

She shivered.

"Ye cold?" He put his arm around her. She tried to shrug it off, but his fingers tightened around her opposite arm. "Dinnae fight me, Wife." He leaned in close for her ears alone. "We're supposed to be married. Or have ye already forgotten?"

"These people might think we're married, but you and I both know we're not," she whispered. "So, keep your hands to yourself, bozo."

"Bozo? What is this bozo?"

Her lips twitched as if she were trying not to laugh. "You."

"I dinnae know what the word means, but I have the impression 'tis an insult."

"You're quick."

Iain winced at her sarcasm. His angel sometimes acted like a witch.

She huffed and sank low, but a moment later, she tilted her head and the light of the fire shone in her eyes. "Haven't you got some sweet girl waiting for you?"

He looked down at his hands. For some reason, he didn't want to tell her about Fiona. It wasn't as if they were formally engaged. Laird MacKinnon had only broached the subject with Iain before he'd left for the war. Iain had said he'd think about it but could see no reason why he and Fiona couldn't be married.

He glanced at Abigail. There was no reason even now to change his mind. However, there was also no reason to mention his possible future engagement. Maeve came to his mind. "I do."

She tensed and tried again to move away. He held her tight.

"If you can't be with the one you love, love the one you're with, is that it?"

"My sister awaits my return."

"Your sister?"

He nodded. "I have left her with much responsibility. 'Tis time for me to take it back off her shoulders."

"Very gallant of you, indeed. Is there no one else?"

"I have not met any lass I have wanted to share my life with." It wasn't a lie, but Iain knew it was only a half-truth. Fiona wasn't a woman he would choose to spend his life with, but sometimes people didn't get to choose.

Abigail would understand such things. Her family might now be in talks for her own arranged marriage, so why didn't he tell her about Fiona? He decided it was too much detail, and he and Abigail would part company soon enough, anyway.

He wasn't sure if it was the light of the fire that colored her face, or a blush that reddened her cheeks. He pushed the stray tendrils of hair behind her ear so he could see her better.

She moved to stand up.

"Where do ye think ye're going?"

"I have to, um . . . take a walk."

His eyebrows shot up at that, and he laughed. "I'll go with ye."

"Ah, no, you will not."

With that, she gently pushed him away, but even so, the jolt had him choking back a groan. The pain had returned without him being aware before that moment.

"Sorry, but some things are private."

He let her go, but as soon as her back was turned, he stood up and followed her. She tottered into the forest, going further than she had need to for privacy, and then disappeared behind a tree.

"I know you're there, so don't go getting any weird ideas."

He smiled. He liked the strange way she spoke. Turning his back to the tree, he called out, "I am a gentleman of honor and I have me back turned."

She mumbled something about honor her butt, and he chuckled. He had come to enjoy her way of speaking, and especially her throwaway lines that should have sounded disrespectful but somehow made him smile.

"Okay," she said from behind, "we can go back now." And she started picking her way out of the forest.

He stood in her path and pulled her into him—close. The scent of the herbal concoction Mary had put through her hair had his nostrils flaring. Even with their clothing between them, he still felt her warmth. "That isn't the way, lass."

"Oh." She gazed up at him, her lips trembling. "Which way, then?"

He dipped his head to his left. "That way."

She fit so perfectly against him, he didn't want to let her go. He touched his lips to her hair.

Her body tensed. She was getting ready to flee.

Inanely, he said, "Yer hair has a hint of cinnamon."

Pushing her hands between them, her palms against his chest, she moved back enough that he felt the loss of her touch. "That was probably in the shampoo Mary gave me."

This was the most challenging conversation he had ever had, but he didn't want to let her go. What was shampoo? He wanted to keep her there, and if talking nonsense did that, then he would talk nonsense. "Shampoo?"

She tilted her head back, her mouth tightening in irritation, but Iain didn't miss the way her eyes darkened as they flickered to his lips and back again.

Without thought, Iain bent down, his lips a breath away from her mouth.

She stiffened and pushed her hands against his chest. "No."

"No?" he grated through his constricted throat.

She pushed, straightening her arms and twisting out of his hold. "No means no."

He knew he stood looking at her stupidly, but with passion-filled blood thundering so loudly in his veins, he couldn't think straight. His dazed brain took in her narrowed eyes. She was trying to look fierce, but he saw the passion curling through her stormy irises. He knew without a doubt that if he persisted, he could kiss her, finally taste her lips.

He let her go. Shaking the cotton from his brain, he wondered if the fever he'd felt coming on earlier had arrived.

Certainly, their meeting was unusual. She was different, exotic, and beautiful.

And it had been a long time since he'd enjoyed a woman's kiss.

Perhaps he wanted to taste, to feel a woman's body in his arms one last time before he either died from his injury or was found and killed by the English or their sympathizers. Even without either of those specters hanging over him, the lass wanted nothing more than to go home. He would soon leave her with her family to never see her again.

He caught her gaze.

It didn't matter. He would not ruin the woman who had saved his life. No. He would not be overcome by her body or her strange but enthralling ways.

CHAPTER 11

Iain stood watching her as if he were deeply interested in her next move.

Abby blinked at him.

She'd said no, but her heart was doing crazy jigs in her chest. She had to fight the current of sizzling electricity still drawing her to him. She had to get away or she would be pleading with him to kiss her.

The thought flitted through her mind that he hadn't ever been told no before. She took in his smoldering eyes, long nose, and square jawline—his broad shoulders and muscled chest. Probably not.

She knew without a doubt that he wanted her, but that was all it was—pure lust. Though she had promised herself she would never rely on a man again, she'd never envisaged being stranded in Scotland of the past, where she needed to depend heavily on a man to survive. But that was just while she was trapped there. At home, she was a successful and independent woman.

She straightened her back and peered at him. Men were unreliable, each and every one of them. She took in a deep breath. That wasn't fair. Just because her last boyfriend wasn't there for her when she needed him didn't mean that all men were untrustworthy.

She screwed up her nose. There was no way she could picture the brawny Highlander running away and leaving her at the mercy of muggers. Iain had fought in a battle, for Pete's sake. Cowards didn't engage in sword fights.

She stared at the ground. If she was lucky, she wouldn't find out what Iain was really like. She would go home and resume her life. She kicked at a pile of wet leaves. Her lonely life. If she was honest, and she tried to be, at least with herself, she had never felt so alive since arriving in 1746.

Her body became engaged whenever Iain was near. Her blood seemed to flow through her veins more easily, and in Mary's company, she was quick to laugh. She hadn't felt so free in a long time. Maybe she'd never truly felt free.

As she stepped into the clearing, Colin's low voice growled, "Fill the buckets with water for breakfast."

Abigail spun around, expecting him to be talking to her, and was about to give him an earful, when she noted it was Iain he was ordering about.

Couldn't the oaf see that Iain was a valiant warrior? He was wounded, for Pete's sake, and he'd been traveling with them without complaint. He'd even helped out around the camp as much as he could with his injury, yet the man had the audacity to be rude to him.

She moved to interfere but hesitated when she saw Iain quickly shake his head at her. He took the buckets and headed to the stream.

Dazed, she wondered where the need to defend him had come from. She caught up to him at the water's edge. "Why didn't you tell him where to go?"

Cocking his head at her words, Iain said, "Where would I tell him to go? This is his family."

"Ah, I mean, why didn't you tell him to lay off . . . no." *Ugh, way to make him think you're completely insane, Abs.* "I mean, you shouldn't let him talk to you like that."

He eyed her for a moment, a slight crease between his brows. "They dinnae need us, but we have need of them. Filling buckets takes no strength, and if it keeps us traveling with them, then so be it."

❧

With no choice but to share Iain's blankets, Abby tried to keep as far away from his heat-filled body as she could. But as the fire waned, the cold Scottish night descended upon her, and she began to shiver. She tried to clench her mouth to stop her teeth from chattering. She could feel the heat coming off Iain's body. So close. NO. She had to keep her distance.

Behind her, Iain growled impatiently, and he pulled her in close, wrapping an arm around her.

As if some sort of primal self-preservation took her over, she sought his body's heat.

When she awoke in the morning, Iain's warm body had disappeared, and a peculiar feeling of disappointment overcame her. She hugged the blanket tighter around her. It wasn't the same. She had to admit, she liked having his strong arms around her, and she liked feeling protected even if it was only from the weather.

She shrugged it off; the only reason he held her was to stop her from freezing to death. He'd probably saved her life. She guessed they were even, then.

Sitting up, she stretched to wake up her muscles and get her blood moving through her veins. Her sleepy gaze flitted over the camp, and she spotted Iain being tended to by Lara on the other side of the rebuilt fire. Abby hurried to them, hoping his injury hadn't become infected.

Lara gazed at his side and clucked like a mother hen. "There, 'tis all clean now, but ye cannae be riding a horse with that wound. Ye'll ride in the cart with yer wife."

Abby tilted her head and regarded him as Lara wrapped some cloth around his waist and helped him put on his saffron shirt. He smiled at Lara, an open, honest smile that made little creases appear at the corners of his eyes and mouth. He obviously liked her.

Abby wished she could do something to make him smile like that at her, instead of the tight smiles that gave Abby the sense he was hiding something, or the other type where it was clear he was laughing at her.

Iain tossed his sword into the cart and helped Abby aboard. At his touch, a shiver ran from the spot where he'd held her arm all the way down her spine. She hated that being close to the Scot made her feel that way. Why couldn't someone from her time have her go all gushy at his touch? She hoped one day a man could make her knees weak, but something told her there would be no other man like Iain.

Abby pushed her thoughts about men away and began folding the blankets into a bundle. She needed to think about how she was going to get the orb back. She didn't like the idea, but she had to make Iain look for Thomas. It would put them in danger, but without the orb, she was stuck in 1746.

A horse neighed startling her back to the present.

The men harnessed the horses to the wagon, and the other horses were saddled and ready to go. Colin and the other men talked together. Abby guessed from their gestures they were deciding which direction to travel.

Iain had apparently refused the wagon, because he mounted the horse he'd ridden the previous day, and they began their day's traveling. Her shoulders dropped in relief. It would be easier to keep away from him.

Mary handed out what was left of the bread and dried beef strips. Abigail waved her hand away. "I'm fine." She didn't want to eat the last of their food.

The older woman pushed the meager meal into Abigail's hands. "We'll stop for more provisions at the next town."

As they bumped along what they called a road, Mary teased Lara about her new marriage with her son. "When am I to expect my first grand-bairn?"

Lara's face instantly turned beet red as she dipped her head and pretended to concentrate on her sewing.

Mary grinned at Abby. "She's a shy one."

Lara looked up, her eyes glinting mischievously. "I'm no' shy. 'Tis just that we thought to keep it secret, but yer son is most virile, Mary. I believe I am already with child."

Mary let out a scream, bent forward, and hugged Lara. "A bairn? When?"

"I'm no' sure. Perhaps in the winter?"

Colin brought his horse close to the wagon. "What is the trouble?"

"Naught, Husband." Mary winked at Lara and smiled so widely, she looked crazed.

Colin raised his brows at her as if he'd find out soon enough and rode to the front of the wagon.

Mary giggled and locked Abby in her gaze. "Are ye enjoying married life, lass? Yer man is something to behold."

Fenella, Mary's mother, had remained quiet, appearing to doze in the corner of the litter, but snapped her eyes up at that moment. "Mary. Ye are a married woman."

"Aye. I am, and a more contented woman ye'll no' find, but I know a strong, capable man when I see one."

Abby followed Fenella's gaze to Iain. Even with his wound paining him, he sat straight-backed with a regal bearing.

Letting out a long sigh, Fenella said, "Aye, he is a man for certain."

Abby had to agree. If she was of this time, she could fall for the hunky Laird MacLaren. She gave an inward shake of her head. She wasn't of this era, and she had to get back to her own time and family before she ended up dead and a part of history.

The three women gazed at Abby with conspiratorial expressions. "Ye have eyes only for ye husband," Fenella said. "Is he as virile as he looks?" She laughed. "I can see from yer eyes that he is in yer heart."

Lara and Mary joined Fenella in her merriment.

Abby felt her own cheeks fill with heat. She giggled, glancing at Iain's regal profile. She hoped Iain hadn't seen whatever the women in the wagon apparently viewed in her eyes.

What was she doing? She couldn't get starry-eyed and swoon over some barbarian. For her own sake, she had to get back to her own time. She wanted to tell the women they were mistaken but, how could she? They thought she and Iain were married and presumably in love. Abby growled inwardly. She hated lying to these wonderful people.

Shouts broke her reverie. A band of dirty, hairy men clad in all different tartans had surrounded the caravan. Abby counted seven, but there could have been more still concealed in the woods.

They were on foot but still outnumbered the caravan's men. Although, seeing the near uncontrolled fury on Colin and his sons' faces, she realized that if the MacDonalds were armed, they would already be fighting. But their weapons were in the back of the wagon, safely wrapped in blankets away from the prying eyes of the English.

Colin tried to talk with the bandits. "Whit is it ye want?"

"Coin," the giant red-haired man who seemed to be the

leader said.

"And yer 'orses," a dark-haired man said.

Tavis stopped the wagon.

"Get oot," one of the long-haired brigands roared at the women.

Abby glared at them. They were huge.

He growled again, "Get oot!"

The red-haired oaf was staring intently at Abby. She lowered her eyes. She didn't have her bag, or the pepper spray she kept there, and they were barbarians with weapons they knew how to use—weapons they enjoyed using.

Mary gazed at Colin. He nodded, tilting his head, indicating they should get off the other side of the wagon.

Keeping Blair under her arm, Mary nudged her daughter-in-law. They jumped over the side and scrambled together in a tight group.

Colin leapt off his horse. The redhead waved his sword at him. Colin held up his hands, showing he had no intention of disobeying the man, and edged along the wagon. "Fenella," he said, holding his hands up to help her to the ground.

As soon as her feet hit the ground, Colin pushed her down, growling, "Go to the women."

Fenella, fear brightening her eyes, crawled under the wagon to the other side.

Redhead roared a laugh. "We dinnae take auld women." His narrow gaze turned to a leer as he eyed Lara.

Parlin dismounted with a thump, taking Redhead's attention off his wife.

Abby hesitated.

She pushed a sword blade back under the blanket with her foot and searched for Iain. He had dismounted but stood close to his horse's side, his eyes full of black anger. Two bandits stood between her and the Scottish laird. She slipped down off the wagon, and Mary pulled her into the huddle.

Tavis also dismounted and stood beside Colin, who untied a bag of coin from his belt. He rested one arm along the side of the wagon as if they were just having a friendly chat, and handed the bag to Redhead, indicating that the others should do the same.

Two of the long-haired rogues sauntered closer to the women. The short black-haired fiend leered at Lara and licked his lips.

Abby glanced at Iain. His jaw was set hard. Something inside Abby told her of all the men she had known, Iain would protect her, but he was too far away, and without a weapon, he had no chance of besting the bandits. Mary tried to push Lara behind her, but the short man shoved Mary to the side so hard, she fell to the ground, a noisy gasp of air escaping from her throat.

He advanced on Lara.

Abby pounced between the girl and the bandit. "Leave her alone."

He laughed.

The other men joined him in laughter.

Catching his breath, Short Man said, "Ye be an eager one."

"Give her what she wants," one of them called.

"Leave the women alone," Colin said. "You have our coin. Go and leave us be."

The taller scummy bandit caught Abby's arm as she tried to help Mary up.

"Nay, this one be mine."

Even at arm's length, his sweaty, unwashed scent soured in her nostrils. She tried to worm her way out of his clutch.

"No' so fast, lass." He jerked her in so close, her back banged on his chest. Something hard caught her shoulder blade. She cried out.

CHAPTER 12

As if his angel's voice was some kind of signal, hot blood pumped through Iain's veins. All the bandits seemed enthralled with what the small bandit was doing. Their laughter grated on Iain's nerves, but keeping his anger in check, he stepped quietly but deliberately toward the wagon.

By their speech, Iain knew they were Scottish Lowlanders, but Lowlanders didn't generally wear the tartan. They could have been Campbell spies, though their mixed tartan dress confused him. Only two were the same, and the thought struck him that they had stolen the tartans or mayhap even plucked the clothes off dead men.

Bloody traitors.

Without taking his eyes off the bandits, he nodded to Colin, who in turn tipped his head to his sons.

Throwing the blanket off his weapon, Iain jerked his sword from its scabbard.

He advanced on the cootie holding Abigail. She fought like a cat, but the boar-like man twisted her arm, his pig nose sniffing her hair. His eyes widened in confusion at her curses, but a mean smile showed blackened teeth.

She cried out again and tried to scratch him with her free hand, but he hit his open hand across her face.

At the man's touch on Abigail, hot angry blood flashed like lightning through Iain's veins. That man dared to lay a hand on her. Iain moved to drag the oaf off her but before he could get close enough, the rest of the bandits ran at him.

Thankful his training included using his left hand as much as his favored right, Iain switched to whatever hand was closest to the nearest bandit. Each jarring connection of blade against blade tore through his chest, causing pain to radiate from his injury. He disarmed the brigands one at a time as they came at him. Colin and his sons joined the fray, and the clang of swords rang through the air.

A young lad stepped in Iain's path. Iain glared at him and lifted his sword. The lad's eyes widened in fear, and he ran from the road into the bracken.

With one more step forward, Iain held Abigail's captor's eyes with his. The man blinked, and Iain whirled, slicing his blade through the air and across the back of the man's hand holding the lass.

The bandit cried out and let go of Abigail. She fell to her knees away from his grasp as he held his bloody hand and glared pure hatred at Iain. Grimacing, the ruffian plunged his good hand into his shirt and whisked out a knife. "Ye want to play hero? Come and play."

Iain frowned. The ejit actually thought he had a chance. A knife against a sword? He was so intent on the confident man, Iain didn't see another bandit fall on him from behind. As the lout wrestled Iain for his blade, Iain kept part of his attention on the one with the knife. The man drew back his arm, ready to throw his weapon.

Iain immediately brought his foot up and kicked his

attacker's groin, hard. The man crumpled forward. Abigail screamed, and Iain ducked, the knife whizzing over his head.

Switching his grip on the hilt of his sword to his good hand, Iain pushed the hurt man aside and strode toward the man who had wielded the knife.

Knife man's eyes darted in all directions, but with no aid at hand, he had the sense to run for his life.

Abigail fell into Iain's chest, and he brought her in close with his sword arm. She sobbed. "It's all right, lassie. Stay here."

Reluctantly, he let her go. He had to get rid of the remaining bandits, before he could comfort the frightened lass.

Colin's roar echoed as he whipped his sword through the air and set on a bandit. The brothers were busy battling the others.

Iain joined them. His adrenaline masked the agony of his injury, but his sword's weight increased with every movement. He had to rid the caravan of the marauders before he collapsed with exhaustion. He rushed the redheaded leader and easily parried the bandit's every attack. The man clearly wasn't an experienced fighter.

He pressed his blade to the man's throat and noted the fear rising in his opponent's eyes.

"Please," the red-haired man pleaded.

Iain huffed and withdrew his sword. "Get oot."

The man fled in the direction his band members had taken earlier.

Realizing they were outmatched, the rest of the bandits followed suit.

With no more opponents, Iain let the tip of his sword fall to the ground. He stood panting in much-needed air, gazing from one caravaner to the other. Colin was the first to break out laughing. His sons hooted and waved their broadswords at the fleeing men's backs.

They were government men. Scottish who fought for the English. He wondered whose orders they were under. Cumberland must have sent them to search out Jacobites. He should have thought; he should have killed them all. But once they'd taken Abigail, he had lost his head. They would know he was a Jacobite and would surely report back. He had put the MacDonalds in danger, and Abigail too.

The bonny lass's eyes did not see him, did not to see anything. The storm had died within her eyes, and confusion swam in its wake.

He tightened his jaw. He had to get her to her family, to safety, and the sooner the better.

CHAPTER 13

Abby was paralyzed as she attempted to process what had just played out before her. She'd dealt with scoundrels, like the man who stole her purse on the street, but she'd never in her entire existence expected to be nearly engaged in a blasted sword fight. Attacking, killing, defending was a way of life for these people.

Those kinds of scenarios belonged in her history texts and enthralling epic fantasy novels. She gazed unseeingly around her. It was far too much for her to fathom. Numbness and inexplicable fear simultaneously pervaded her emotions, one doing its best to overcome the other. It was a dreadful combination and she was left feeling exposed and inadequate.

Abigail searched out Iain. He pierced her with his gaze, waking up her numb body. She ran to him and flung her arms around his waist.

He brought her in close. His strength, not just physical but emotional, propped her up, fortifying her shaking legs and calming her breaths. Her heart still beat too quickly, but the rhythm altered, and instead of it rearing up in fright, it pattered like butterfly wings in her chest.

He rested his chin on the top of her head and stroked her hair to where it was caught in the braid. The tips of his fingers lightly brushed her neck at each pass, sending electric thrills through her body.

Iain's hand moved from her side to her lower back. The charge increased as shivers ran down Abigail's back. His fingers spread over her skin.

Everyone crowded around Iain and Abigail. "Go on," Colin said. "Kiss yer wife."

Iain let out a noisy frustrated breath and, kissing the top of her head, moved apart from her.

The men slapped Iain on the back and thanked him for his bravery and skill.

Abigail reluctantly stepped back to allow them room for their greetings.

The women hugged and kissed him. Abby wasn't overly keen on the women kissing Iain, but she agreed wholeheartedly that he was a fine, brave man.

She'd been so scared when the bandit grabbed her. She'd thought she would have to save herself again. She'd thought no one would come to her aid. Why would they imperil themselves for someone they didn't know?

Her own boyfriend, in what now seemed like a previous life, had left her alone to fend off a gang of youths, intent on stealing whatever valuable she had. Peter fled from the park as Abby cried out his name.

She hadn't even called out to Iain, but he, an injured Scotsman, roared at the man who manhandled her. Iain's eyes had flashed with dark fury as he bore down on the bandit with his sword. He had cut the man's hand where he'd held Abby and chased the rogues away with his fierceness. Yet, he had not made her any promises. She was not his to protect, yet he fought for her like she was his own.

Tears burned Abby's eyes at both scenes. One filled her

with angry hurt, and the other overwhelmed her with emotion.

Iain gazed intently at Abby. She wiped her eyes, refusing to let the tears flow. Something hard and cold sparked in Iain's gaze. "Are you hurt?"

She shook her head. "No."

⚜

After a celebratory feast of dried meat, bread, and watery wine, Iain built a smaller fire away from the main one. He covered the ground with a blanket and stretched his body out full-length upon it.

"Come here, Wife."

His twisted smile was downright sexy, and it sent excited shivers crawling all over Abby. She glanced at her newfound friends. Mary smiled at her and then returned her attention to her husband.

With dark—*sultry* was the only word that came to Abby's mind at that moment—eyes, Iain held up another blanket and shook it. "Wife."

She couldn't refuse, nor did she want to. She took the blanket, sat beside him, and pulled it over both their bodies.

"Thank you for today," she said.

He pulled her down onto her back as he rolled onto his uninjured shoulder and stared at her. His eyes flitted from her forehead to her eyes to her nose and lingered on her lips. She bit back an excited gasp. The fire softened the burgeoning beard on his face but flashed orange in his irises. Before she knew what was happening, he brought his lips down on hers. She opened her mouth in surprise, and he took full advantage.

Abby's brain clouded, and a low roar buzzed in her ears. Her mouth opened wider, and her arms slithered around him, her hands splaying across his hard, broad back. She wanted to get as close to him as she could. She wanted to push her body right into his. Heat like a sunny Californian day seeped through his muscled back and straight into her arms. His whole body was afire. Her skin burnt with passion as a deep well of desire fueled her core.

A voice screamed in her head, *Stop him!* Although the logical part of her brain knew he was only kissing her to make a show of their love for the benefit of the MacDonalds, she was enjoying it way too much. She couldn't let it go on any longer, so she tried to end the kiss without making a scene.

But he deepened the kiss.

She dug a fingernail in the crook of his neck.

He let her go and sputtered. "What did ye do that for?"

"Shh." Abby glanced at the wagon. There was no movement. "Remember?" she whispered. "I said no funny business."

Iain growled. "It is no funny, no at all."

"Well no one's looking at us any more, so there's no reason to continue pretending."

He regarded her for a moment and while a hint of desire still clouded his eyes, he acquiesced and moved back.

Abby thought she heard a soft sigh but couldn't make out his features in the dark to see his expression. Before she could say anything, he rolled his back to her.

She snuggled down beside him, trying to keep a gap between their bodies. Having to keep up the pretense she was married to Iain was unleashing feelings she didn't want to feel. She had to go back home, and Iain had to return to his home. There was no way they could get involved, even if it was only physical. It would be wrong, so, so wrong.

Abby awoke during the night with Iain throwing his hands about and rolling his head from side to side. He shouted something in ancient Gaelic. She placed her hand on his cheek. No wonder he felt so hot during the kiss; he was burning up. How could she not have noticed? And now he could be getting delirious.

She quickly filled a bucket with ice-cold loch water and, dunking in a clean cloth, began wiping Iain's now-sweating face. She cooed soft calming noises close to his ear as she worked.

After about twenty minutes of her ministrations, he settled enough to sleep quietly. Exhausted, Abby slept, too, but it wasn't long before Iain began thrashing about again.

Three times during the night, Iain's fever sent him into some horrible nightmare. Abby did what she could, cooling his skin and soothing him with her voice, but each time, his convulsions, if that was what they were, got longer. The last time, somewhere close to dawn, it had taken Abby over an hour to calm him enough that he slept somewhat peacefully again.

Once the morning showed up disguised as dark clouds, she made up her mind. It was too risky to travel in an open wagon. She had to find somewhere dry and warm where she could tend Iain until he was well. She refused to let the flickering thought of him dying take hold in her mind.

The night before rose unbidden in her thoughts. The rush of passion as his skin touched hers had to be because of her heightened emotions, because she was scared and so out of her depth in that time. She was terrified that if she stayed any longer, she would either lose her mind or her heart. Neither was a scenario she wanted.

She gazed at him. She would make him well again, get the device back, and go home.

Abby put the wet cloth on his forehead. If only she could get him to a modern doctor. He needed antibiotics. What could she do? Nothing but make him comfortable and watch and wait. It was ridiculous. She shook her head. If she had the blasted time device, she could take him home, guarantee his safety.

He could die, and she would be alone. In this era, people died more often than not with the smallest ailments.

She decided to rebuild the main fire so at least he would be warm.

"You look terrible," Mary said at the sight of her. "Are ye sick?"

"I'm not, but my husband has a fever." Abby looked up at the threatening sky. "We need to find somewhere dry. Even if he stayed in the wagon, the jostling would cause him pain."

Colin and his sons were already packing up the wagon. Mary stood up and put her hand on Abby's arm. "You must stay with us until we get to Inverell. There be doctors there. It is too dangerous out here."

The day before exploded in Abby's mind. Mary was right; she couldn't very well haul Iain across the country alone in the hopes that they would find somewhere to shelter. As if to cement that assumption, rain began to fall. She gave a slight shake of her head. At least the canvas wagon cover would keep them dry. A stuffy wagon was better than staying out in the miserable weather alone.

Abby ducked her head yes. "Thank you."

Colin and his youngest son, Tavis, carried Iain to the wagon, and Abby poked as many blankets as she could under Iain to help cushion the wagon's jerky movements.

It rained steadily all morning, and Abby watched the isolated country pass by.

She was about to give up searching for a likely building, when she spotted something some distance to the left of the road. "What's that?" She pointed to what looked like a dilapidated farm building of sorts.

Mary peered into the distance. "Nay. Ye have to stay until we get to Inverell so ye can get a doctor for the lad."

Iain moaned. "Nay,"...mumble..."Inverell . . . Cumberland."

Looking from Iain to Abby, Mary nodded. "Aye, there will be English there for certain." She felt Iain's forehead. "Mayhap ye can stop his fever, but if ye cannae, he weel die."

Iain grabbed Abby's hand. "Must leave."

Abby didn't know what to do. If they stayed with the MacDonalds, the English would catch them for sure and the family themselves would be in danger, but if she left with Iain, he could die.

Colin talked to Mary quietly at the end of the cart, and once he'd left, Mary pulled some plants from a small box and handed them to Abby.

"This one is Peruvian bark from France, and this is willow bark. Boil them in water and feed it to him on the hour. Ye must do this until the fever breaks."

Abby smiled. She could do that. "Thank ye," she said, using the Scottish term for *you* without thinking.

Lara handed Abby a small bottle of cream. "It is a lotion made from carline thistle. Put it on ye man's wound to ease the infection."

"Very good, Lara, I had forgotten about that," Mary said, and then she called out, "Stop the cart."

Once Tavis brought the cart to a stop, all except Iain hopped out of the wagon, and Mary frowned at Abigail. "Be careful, child, and do as we say."

Abby nodded. "I will."

They hugged and said goodbye. "I hope I see ye again," Mary said.

"Me too," Lara said, giving Abigail a bag of food.

Abigail gazed inside, tears welling in her eyes. "This is too much."

"Nay," Mary said. "Colin and the lads weel hunt now that we are in the hills. There's plenty of game aboot."

Giving her a one-armed hug, Abigail said, "Thank you for your kindness."

Colin and his sons carried Iain to the rundown building. Tavis helped Abigail drag out a cot from a side room and place it in the main room. It was the only room with a fireplace. Actually, it was a hole in the ground in the middle of the room, but Abby recognized it as a fire pit. A great kettle hung to the side from a chain attached to the roof. A pot and a griddle rested against the back wall.

Colin and Parlin placed Iain on the cot with as many blankets as they could spare, and once they'd started the fire, they left. Abby was once again alone with the Scot.

She gazed at the man and willed him to get well and wake up.

CHAPTER 14

I ain woke. His head ached as if someone had hit him with an axe head. His blurry sight had him wondering if he'd had sand thrown into his eyes. He blinked, but his eyelids ached with the movement. That small movement sent a quaking throughout his body, every nerve screaming at the intrusion.

He stilled and concentrated his focus.

Reward.

Through his hazy vision, he could see his angel dozing in an old chair. Her long hair fell loose about her as she lay with her hands under the side of her head resting on the arm of the chair. He smiled at her pink kissable mouth. She was a bonny lass. She had taken off her cloak and used it to cover her body. The memory of his arms around those curves sent tingles down his spine.

He dragged his gaze from her and looked about. They were in an old farmhouse, and he was in a bed. The smell of peat fire filled the room, but he heard no other sounds. They were alone. Any other time, he would be thankful, but with the English army and their Scottish allies scouring the High-lands for Jacobites, they were in danger.

Even if he was well and healthy, they would be at a disad-vantage, but with his body aching and his fevered mind still swirling in confusion, he couldn't even lift a sword. He couldn't protect her. Whether asleep or awake, protecting her was all he'd thought about since the attack on the MacDon-alds' group.

If any of their enemies found them, Abigail would be at their mercy. Knowing how they would treat her, his heart lurched. He shouldn't have let the MacDonalds leave them there. He should have fought for the lass's safety.

But no, he wasn't thinking clearly. They couldn't go to Inverell. They would have put the entire family in danger for being associated with a Jacobite fighter. He frowned. He should have insisted Abigail stay with the MacDonalds. He'd had fevers before. He could have slept through the worst of the heat, and once it had broken, if it broke and he lived, he could have been on his way to Dorpol. Alone, he would have covered more ground faster.

One of Abigail's feet fell out from under her cloak. The material slipped, exposing a long, naked leg. And a more perfect leg he had never seen. He knew he should, but he couldn't drag his eyes off her. His mouth went dry and heat rose through his body. He choked back a gasp

Iain peered closer. She wasn't wearing her skirt. Mayhap she thought he was still too feverish to notice.

A heaviness set in his aching eyelids, but he forced them to stay open. He didn't want to stop looking at her, for she still looked like an angel to his eyes. He was also scared she might turn out to be a fever vision after all and disappear. Had they even traveled with the MacDonalds? Was it all a dream and he was still on the battlefield, slowly dying?

Iain fisted his hand and dug his fingernails into his palm. Nay. He was in a deserted house with the most beautiful lass he had ever set his eyes on.

Her eyes blinked open and caught his. She gasped and sat up, wiping her mouth. "You're awake."

"Aye." His voice was gritty. The corners of his mouth twitched.

Abigail threw her cloak off, jumped up, and bent forward to feel his forehead. "You're still hot."

His eyes widened at the open top of her shirt.

She stood up and scrunched the material closed.

Raking his gaze over her near-naked body, he cleared his throat and winced. "That isn't going to make much difference."

Her eyes widened, and she looked down. She gasped in surprise. Had she forgotten her state of undress?

She had dispensed with the skirt and vest and only wore a shirt. Iain couldn't remember seeing anything like her shirt's style before. It was long enough to cover her body but not much else. He couldn't place the cloth, but it was as shiny as silk. Mayhap it *was* silk. He frowned at the buttons. They were small and white but not covered in cloth, and they were placed from neck to hem. It wasn't like any sark or shift he had ever seen.

She glared at him. "Stop looking at me like that."

He raised his eyebrows, his eyes roaming down her length once more.

"Blast it. Turn away so I can get dressed."

"I like it." He grinned, knowing hunger eclipsed the pain in his eyes. By the boar's blood, his whole body hungered for her.

She snatched up her skirt and, turning her back to him as if she thought that would give her privacy, she bent forward to step into the skirt. His breath hitched in his throat as the bottom of her shirt rose. Something pink and shiny that again looked like silk covered her skin but was so tight, he had nothing to compare it to. Who, what was she? If he was going to die in the rundown farmhouse, he wanted to know more about her first.

She wrenched the skirt up over her long legs and tied it at her waist.

As she turned back to him, she held out her arms and sang, "Ta da."

Taken aback, Iain stared at her.

She let out a small laugh. "Don't worry about it. It's just an expression from where I'm from."

Although he was sorry to see her so covered, he decided it was for the best.

He patted the bed. "Tell me aboot ye, yer family, yer country."

He gritted his teeth and made room for her but couldn't stop a groan from escaping his throat from the movement.

"Keep still." Abigail filled a mug with water and set it down on the small round table beside the bed.

She leaned so close, he could smell the faintest glow of herbs and breathed in her sweetness as she propped up the folded blanket, she had placed behind him. He helped as much as his weakened body allowed, which wasn't much at all. Abigail grunted with the effort, and by the time she had him in a semi-upright position, she was panting.

His voice rasped, "Thank ye."

"Thank me by drinking this."

He glowered at the mug. He didn't want to drink. The last time she made him take some water, his stomach had twisted in excruciating pain. He glanced up at her hopeful face. If he wanted to have strength to do all the things his fevered mind imagined, he needed to drink.

Placing the mug against his cracked lips, she waited for

him to bend his head to it before tipping it up. He drank a mouthful and then pulled away. A rope pulled the water down into his gut and thrashed about for painful moment.

When it passed, he said, "I am much indebted to ye, angel."

"I'm not an angel, and don't think twice about it."

He tilted his head. He hadn't thought twice, and he only spoke once.

She picked at a loose thread in her skirt. "I can't go anywhere at the moment, anyway. Actually, I'm glad to have your company. I don't know what I'd do here all by myself."

"Ye should have stayed with the MacDonalds."

She rolled her eyes to the ceiling. "And have Tavis continually trying to help me and hanging off my every word?"

His newly bearded jawline twitched in anger. Had Tavis been so forthright to a married woman? "Did he—"

Abigail's eyes widened. "What? No. He's just a kid . . . a lad."

"He's old enough to marry."

"He's not old enough to marry me, and anyway, he and his whole family thought"—she pointed to Iain and then to herself—"we were already married."

"Ye should have told me."

She ducked her head and her hands shook as she straightened the blanket over him. She smiled. "I've read about you Highland types."

"Aye? What have you read?"

"You are all womanizers. What do you call it? Wenching, that's it. You all go around wenching."

He laughed, but a cough quickly followed. He held up a hand. "Don't be jesting. It hurts me to laugh." He gave her his best smoldering smile. "Women do have a penchant for a handsome Highlander."

"Like you?"

"Do you think I'm handsome then?"

She scoffed and shook her head, turning her gaze away as if seeing something other than a stone wall. "It doesn't matter what I think."

"Aye. It matters."

Had he seen a spark in her eyes before she averted her gaze? Aye. He had. She was having sinful thoughts as much as he was. That kiss the last night with the MacDonalds had sent his body into a whir, and he was sure she felt the same.

He drew his brows together. But that was after he had saved her. She could have merely been thankful. It might have been her appreciation that she had showed him.

She went over to the pot over the fire. "I've made a broth with the oats and meat Mary gave us."

Iain thought perhaps he could beat this fever. He smashed his lips together. Unlikely. He had seen fever take many. The heat spared no one—warriors, men, women, or bairns.

Why the hell did he have to meet her when he was near death?

Why couldn't he have met her when he was a brawny, healthy man, a man, lasses admired?

All he wanted was to kiss her. He hardened his jaw. If he wanted the chance to have Abigail in his arms, he needed his strength.

Iain tried to eat as much of the broth as he could, but the act of swallowing made him gag. The effort weakened his already feeble body. He groaned a small, frail noise no man would want to have the bonniest lass in the world hear.

Abigail ignored his distress and continued to pour the brew down his throat. As if her speaking would take Iain's mind off his discomforts, she spoke of her family. Names Iain found as strange as she was. Max, Garrett, and Izzy.

"Max tried to teach me and Izzy to fight, but we'd all end up laughing because we couldn't do what she said."

Iain spluttered and fell back, the broth spilling over the rim onto his chest. Max was a she? What sort of name was that for a lass?

"Max is your sister?"

Abigail nodded and laughed. "Maxine. Only my sister could get away with some of the things she's done to me."

She wiped Iain's wet chest with a cloth and sighed as she returned the bowl to a spot near the fire.

He frowned. She didn't appear to be in any hurry to return to him.

He already missed the sound of her voice. If he was to die that night, he wanted to hear her voice as he left the mortal world. With what little strength he had, he asked softly, "What else did your sister do to you?"

She turned fearful eyes on him but nodded and sat down.

He knew then she was afraid of him dying and leaving her to fend for herself in what must be a strange and frightening land. "Tell me more about Max," he said.

She shrugged and said, "One time, she built a trap in the backyard for us. It was a big cage. Where she got it from, she still won't tell me, but anyway, she rigged up the cage so the open end was up off the ground, and she covered the top with leaves and the sides with branches so we couldn't see it for what it was.

Plates of candies . . . ah, sweets and cakes were on a small table under the cage. Izzy and I were on them in a second, but no sooner had we popped the sweets into our mouths, then the cage crashed down around us."

Abigail giggled and shook her head. "Izzy screamed so loud, Garrett came running, but when he saw our predicament, he fell to the ground, laughing so hard he couldn't talk. At least that stopped Izzy from screaming. I knew Max was the culprit. I called for her, and she said from the top of the cage, 'You should be more aware of your surroundings.' She jumped down, and once Garrett pulled himself together, they lifted the cage off us.

"Max continued to lecture us on how we should notice when things changed in our surroundings while we ate all the sweets and cakes."

Iain couldn't imagine how Garrett came to be in pieces and how he had to pull himself together, but he didn't question her strange words. He wanted to keep her talking. He licked his lips and moved his tongue around in his mouth for lubrication. "Was there a reason for her worrying about ye?"

"I suppose. Our parents were rich and had a lot of priceless stuff in the house. She was always reading stories about rich kids getting kidnapped and held for ransom, or how thieves broke into houses and threatened families." She smiled wistfully. "Max was always wanting to fight the bad guys, but I wish she didn't have to use us as practice so much."

"Aye, sisters can be menaces."

"What sort of things has your sister done to you?"

"When she heard I was going to join Bonnie Prince Charlie's army, she had me locked in the dungeon."

"What? Really? How did you get out?"

"I threatened to announce her marriage to Murry."

"Murry?"

He let out a weak laugh. "Murry is an old hermit who lives in solitude in a cave on the beach."

"And could you have made her marry him?"

"Aye, all I had to do was announce the betrothal and it would be done."

Her tinkling laughter had Iain smiling. "That was really mean, but I can understand why you did it. Sisters can be the worst sometimes."

"Aye."

Iain wanted to hear more about her family, but her visage blurred as blackness seeped into his brain. He fought it, ignoring his aching body's plea to sleep. He didn't want to leave her. He blinked and refocused.

He felt they had forged a connection with their stories. He wished he could concentrate, ask more questions. His entire body ached, and the blackness was encroaching from the edges of his mind. He threw his head from side to side, trying to rid his mind of the sinister stuff.

She dipped the cloth into water and placed it on his forehead, putting a hand on his chest to still him. "For Pete's sake, will you stay still?"

Iain relaxed. His angel's hand felt like ice on his burning skin as she ran her palm across his brow. He shut his eyes at the momentary relief.

"Please," Abigail said, her voice barely above a whisper. "Sleep."

She shivered and glanced at the sputtering fire. "I'll put some more peat on the fire."

He forced his aching lids open and was rewarded with the view of her hips swaying as she walked to the wall, collected the blocks, and bent to feed the fire. She stood up, rubbing her arms.

Iain couldn't feel the cold, but he knew the night would be freezing.

Returning to the pallet, she drew up his kilt and tucked it in around him.

"You're cold. You take it."

"I have blankets."

Picking up the side of the covers, Iain grinned. "Perhaps we can both be warm this night."

A pink flush grew in her cheeks as she seemed to be weighing his suggestion.

She offered him a shy smile but shook her head. "No, it'll only make you hotter, and we have to bring the fever down, not make it worse."

He sighed, knowing she was right. Closing his eyes, he hoped she would keep him company in his dreams.

CHAPTER 15

Abby awoke to Iain thrashing from side to side. Shaking the sleep from her brain, she sat on the side of the bed as he grated out words, mumbles, really, she couldn't decipher.

The cold air brought goose pimples out on her arms, but he was so hot and sweaty. She shivered and wrapped her now dry cloak around her, noticing the fire had died down. She quickly threw more peat into the fire until flames began to warm the room once more. The morning light was gray . . . again.

Before the heavens opened, Abby hurried to the stream and fetched another bucket of water, all the while wondering if she should have made Iain swallow as much broth as she did the night before. Maybe she had made him even sicker. What was the old saying? Feed a cold, starve a fever or feed a fever, and starve a cold? She had a worrying hunch that it was the former. *Great. Way to go, Abby.*

Back in the house, she scrubbed strips of cloth as well as she could and stretched them out by the fire to dry before taking off her shirt and underwear and washing them. She hoped they would dry before Iain awoke. She paused. If Iain awoke. No. She wouldn't think like that. He had to survive. He had to get better, and soon.

She wrung a cloth out in the freezing water and began bathing him with it. She wiped his face, neck, chest, and as far down as she dared. As she redressed his wound, she was certain the infection was lessening. The redness around the edge of the wound was gone, and it wasn't as swollen as the night before. *Please let him be all right. Please.*

Between bouts of crazed shouting and thrashing around on the bed, Iain dove into unconsciousness. No matter what state he was in, however, the fever racked his body. How he could be so hot and look so blue as if he were freezing, she didn't know, but it worried her. The only thing she could do was wash him with the wet cloths and pray.

She wasn't a religious person, but she believed in a higher power, a place where the deceased crossed over. Abby just hoped it wasn't Iain's time to go to that place. She was just getting to know him, and she liked him. A lot, if she was honest with herself.

She reheated the meat broth and boiled the kettle. She made a mug of Mary's tea for herself and a bowl of Mary's herbal tea for Iain.

Forcing herself to eat, she watched the rise and fall of Iain's massive chest. His face had relaxed somewhat, and his mouth hung open a little in what looked like a peaceful sleep.

She put her bowl down and, whipping another cloth out of the bucket of cold water, she squeezed out most of the water. With it still dripping a little, she placed it over his forehead. He groaned but this time, he didn't appear to be in pain. It was more a happy groan, if there was such a thing.

She wiped the cloth down over his face and neck and opened it out over his chest. The short black curls coiled tighter as they moistened. In a circular motion, she rubbed gently.

Feeling watched, her gaze darted to his face. He was awake, and his lips were slanted in a sexy smile. Her hands froze.

"You're awake." Stupid. Of course he was. Did she always have to state the obvious?

"Aye."

Feeling his forehead with the back of her hand, her heart flipped. The fever was gone. "You don't have a fever."

His eyes slid down her throat and widened. "Nay."

She glanced down and pulled her cloak together. "Stay there."

He chuckled. "Aye."

She scooped up her shirt and hurried to a shadowed corner of the room. Facing the corner, she said over her shoulder, "Turn your head away."

"Nay."

Figuring he wouldn't see much, anyway, Abigail quickly disposed of the cloak and pulled the shirt over her head. When she turned around, Iain was trying to sit up.

Pushing him back against the blanket roll, she said, "What did I tell you? Stop moving, you stubborn man."

Removing the dressing from his side, she was amazed at how good the wound looked. She wiped off the cream Lara had given her but decided not to replace it with more. "I'm going to let the wound dry out before redressing it."

"Aye."

He sat up and examined his injury. "Ye have saved me life, Abigail. I thank ye."

"Don't thank me yet."

She picked up the bowl of broth and began to spoon feed him.

He took the bowl from her. "I can do that meself."

Once he'd finished, she tried to give him more of the herbal tea.

"Nay. I don't need that witches' brew any longer."

"I think you do. Drink it."

"Nay."

Abby couldn't believe how childish he was acting. "If you don't want to relapse, you'll drink the darn tea."

"But it is hideous."

She smelt it and screwed up her nose. "Well, yeah, but it's good for you. Now drink."

He cocked his head and made a face. "Only for you, angel."

She was going to tell him not to call her an angel again but decided now wasn't the time for any more arguments.

As soon as he finished the tea, he fell into an exhausted but peaceful sleep. Abby was amazed at the rate of his recovery. He was incredibly strong.

She put on her cloak and collected the herbal shampoo-like stuff Mary and Lara had given her. Excited to finally bathe, she couldn't wait to use the amazingly perfumed shampoo all over her entire body.

Sunlight lit up the grounds around the house. She tipped her head back and smiled. The sun warmed her face, but only slightly. She hoped it stayed out while she washed in the stream. She figured she had some time before Iain woke up again.

When she'd finished and made her way back to the house, she felt the cleanest she had since she left her family home. She hummed as she pulled on her clean underwear. Even her dirty skirt and vest couldn't stifle her mood. She was clean, Iain was on the road to recovery, and they would soon be on their way to get her orb back.

She'd only just sat down again when Iain opened his eyes. "Hello."

His voice was harsh from dryness, but Abby had never heard anything so beautiful. Although he was still weak, he insisted he was strong enough to go outside.

He swung his legs over the side of the bed and, pulling a blanket around his waist, he stood up.

He seemed so much taller under the low ceiling . . . and wider. His arm muscles flexed as he tightened his grip on the blanket. Abby's eyes popped wide, but she caught herself and averted her face. Whisking his cream shirt off the floor where she had it drying, she kept her head turned as she jabbed it in his general direction.

"I don't need that."

"You do if you want me to stay here."

"Och. Have you never seen a naked man before?"

"I've seen plenty." *None like you, though.* She turned her back to him. "Just put the shirt on, will you?"

He took it from her hand. "You can look now."

She turned. He stood tall. The shirt fell to his knees, and Abby couldn't help her gaze sliding down to his feet and back up again. Were all Highlanders so big? If he was in her time, he would be cast as one of the Greek gods in those fantasy movies. Thor, maybe.

Heat rushed into her face, and she snapped her head up. His smile was downright sexy and had her knees turning to jelly. Quickly sitting down, she grabbed the poker and prodded the fire around.

"I'll take a bucket of water with me." He chuckled and went outside.

The lightness in his voice didn't fool Abby. His legs shook with the effort of hauling the bucket, and she gnawed her bottom lip at the sight of his flushed face. He might think he had the strength of a healthy man, but he was still weak and too ill to be wandering about unaided. What if he fell? Her mind seesawed back and forth. Should she go with him or not? But she decided he needed some privacy, so she stayed inside, busying herself by cleaning as best she could.

When he came back, he seemed more in control of his limbs.

"The fresh air helped me."

He stretched out on the bed and Abby propped up the blankets behind his back.

"Thank ye, lass."

Before she knew it, Iain had closed his hand around the back of her neck and brought her lips down to meet his.

She squirmed out of his grasp before their lips met. "We... we need to go before the English come."

He drew his brows together and said, "Ye have the right of it."

She only wanted to make him better but was worried any undue exertion might set him back. She hoped with all her might he would soon be capable of leaving the area. The constant threat of the English finding them weighed on her every waking moment.

Abby knew she had to deal with getting out of there before someone found them, but right at that moment, she wished she had let Iain kiss her.

Her whole body was on fire, and if he tried to get close to her to kiss her again, she wouldn't be able to resist him.

She gazed up at the blackened ceiling. Why the hell shouldn't she have him? She would never get another chance to be with a hunky Highlander like him.

Because it's not right, Abby. She grimaced at the voice in her head and returned her gaze to Iain. He watched her with no expression whatsoever on his face. Confusion had her mind whirling. The voice continued to intrude on her enjoyment. *You must leave him.*

With an inward sigh, she pulled her hair back and tied it with one of the strips of cloth.

He gazed at her, disappointment washing over his face. "Aye. I understand." He threw his legs off the bed with a grunt. "Ye have to get back to yer family."

He slowly and methodically started packing up the few belongings they had. "I have my family to return to as well."

Abby wanted to tell him he didn't understand. She wanted to tell him the truth, but she couldn't risk it. He could have her burnt at the stake for being a witch.

CHAPTER 16

I ain couldn't understand the woman. He was sure she was as attracted to him as he was her. He was enamored by her, but his feelings for her went deeper than just wanting her physically. He enjoyed his time with her, talking to her, listening to her.

He wanted to know more about the wonderful Abigail, everything, both physically and emotionally. She was a puzzle, but she was no angel. He knew that the moment she kissed him. She had wanted that kiss as much as he had.

His body had never reacted to a woman like it did with her. His mind too seemed to turn to peat moss just at the sound of her voice.

As they worked, Iain's gaze kept returning to Abigail. Mayhap he was too hasty; mayhap she needed more time.

He tore his gaze from her. She was right; they had more important things to see to than letting their physical attraction to one another get in the way.

He had to get to Dorpol. He had to get to his lands before the English did their worst. His sister needed him. He'd left the weight of seeing to the keep and crofters to her for too long now. He also had to make up his mind about Fiona MacKinnon. If he married her, the merging of two clans could only be a good thing for his clan. They needed strength, and the MacKinnons had that in abundance.

Standing and moving to the door, Iain said, "I thought I heard a horse neighing last night. I will see if I can find it."

Abigail tilted her head and gazed at him with serious eyes. "I can't ride a horse."

"There are no horses in your land?"

"Yeah, some people, like my sisters and brother, ride them, but I don't."

"Dinnae fash yersel. I haven't found one yet."

Drinking in one last look at the beautiful lass, Iain made his way outdoors and into the sunshine. The sky was clear, and spring was quickly turning into summer. He spotted a horse nibbling on the new spring grass next to the burnt-out stables.

The horse wasn't in the best condition, but he was strong enough to carry the two of them. He couldn't find a usable saddle, but he found a bridle, and once he'd mended the reins, the horse was set to go.

Abigail had rolled as much food as they could carry in three blankets, and he couldn't help leaning into her clean smell as he took the roll from her.

She didn't seem to notice and was frowning up at the horse's back where Iain had draped a blanket over its whithers.

Iain clasped his hands around her small waist. "Ready?"

"As ready as I'll ever be, I guess."

With one movement, Iain plopped her onto the horse. Iain leapt up and sat behind her. The horse moved, and Abigail let out a cry. Iain wrapped his arm around her waist and pulled her back into his chest. "I'll not let ye fall. Just relax and let yer body go with the horse's movements."

Hanging on to the horse's mane, Abigail hissed through her teeth, "I'll try."

At first, she appeared to handle sitting on the horse well, but after a few miles, she kept shifting her bottom. "If you don't stop doing that, we'll have to stop."

"Sorry, but my butt is really sore."

He chuckled. He loved her way of speaking, and without thinking, he kissed her neck. "Relax."

She stiffened, and he could have hit himself. *Let her be.*

They rode in silence from that point on, and by midafternoon, Iain was ready to rest.

A line of smoke plumed up into the clear sky ahead of them.

"Look," Abigail said, pointing to the dark cloud.

"Aye." Iain stopped the horse.

"Keep going." She turned her head, and her blue eyes darkened in sadness. "There might be someone in trouble there."

She was right, but if the English were responsible for the fire, they might still be there. Iain nudged the horse into a walk, ready to turn and run at the first sign of trouble.

The closer they got, an aroma drifted on the breeze into Iain's nostrils. He had smelled that stench before. Burnt wood and supplies. The aroma was sweet and pungent at the same time.

Abigail gagged and twisted to face him. "What is that smell?"

At that moment, they rounded the bend, and Iain couldn't keep the gasp from escaping his throat. Colin's caravan had been attacked, and by the looks of the wreckage, the MacDonalds had lost everything.

Abigail snatched her head around. "No!"

Iain stopped the horse and dismounted. "Stay here."

But before he'd finished speaking, Abigail had slid off the

horse and stood staring at the scene, her mouth open in shock and horror. She pulled her skirt up over her mouth and nose. "No," she whispered, and began sobbing into the material.

Iain turned her so that her back faced the carnage. He wanted to protect her from seeing the burnt-out wagons, and he had no way of knowing if anybody was killed, but they had to pass to continue their journey. He hugged her to him. "Stay here."

She nodded, and he strode to the site. He couldn't find any friends alive or dead, but Colin or one of his sons had struck one of the attackers down. Iain growled at the colors the murderer wore.

Abigail stopped at his side. Tears streamed down her face. "That's one of Cumberland's men," she said, staring at the bloody carcass.

"Aye."

She turned her face up to his. "Iain, they are going after all Jacobites. They mean to kill all of you."

Iain put his hand on Abigail's shoulder. "I cannae find any MacDonalds. Mayhap they escaped."

Abigail brushed her tears away and beamed at Iain. "Of course, they did. They are a strong family."

"Iain? Abigail?"

Iain turned at Mary's voice, and Abigail was already hugging the woman.

"You're alive," Abigail said, moving back and gazing at Mary.

"Aye, and so too are ye."

They laughed and hugged again as Colin walked up to them.

"How did ye get away?" Iain asked.

"Where are the others?" Abigail asked before Colin could reply.

"They are all safe. We came back to see if there was anything we could salvage."

Iain gazed at the carnage. "I am sorry, but it doesn't appear as if they left anything unbroken or unburned."

"No matter. We have the horses and some supplies, enough to get us to Inverell. Will you join us?"

"No," Mary said. "The men who did this are going there. I heard the leader, Thomas was his name, say that after they report to Inverell, he is going to Rum to find Laird MacLaren. You, Iain. He said if he can't get you, he will have your sister."

Abigail put her hand over her mouth and stared at Iain.

He grunted. "Thomas was always a sore loser. He will not have either me or my sister."

Iain and Colin left Abigail and Mary there and quickly began collecting what they could find of the MacDonald's possessions, and after hurried goodbyes, Iain held Abigail as they watched Colin and Mary disappear over the knoll.

If he was to die at the hands of the English, he would die fighting, but he had Abigail to consider. He tightened a protective arm around her waist. He would do anything to keep this angel safe, but he had to get to Dorpol and Maeve. They must get to Rum and then to the MacLaren Keep.

Abigail shifted her weight and spoke into his shoulder. "How far is Rum?"

"Weeks. The weather is warming and crossing the mountains will shorten our travel to mayhap two weeks. But we need to stay off the main roads on our way there, so that will add many days."

She seemed to sag at his words. "That's a long time. If my family finds me, I will be leaving you before I see your island."

"Aye." Iain didn't want to think about that. He had been trying to find a way to make her stay with him but couldn't think of one.

"I know the government army is looking for all Jacobites, but why do you think they are after you in particular?"

The memory of the shock and fury on the Cumberland knight's face when Iain cut off his ear had him smiling. "Perhaps it's because I sliced off one of Cumberland's officer's ears."

"You what? Don't say it again. Who?"

"Sir Thomas Sutherland. He was at Glasgow University at the same time I was, and he was always a mean one. I caught him more than once beating into one of the first-year lads."

Iain blew out a breath at the memory. No matter how many times Iain bested the man at fisticuffs, he wouldn't change his ways. "He is one of many traitors belonging to the Independent Highland Company. They are no more than militia, bought and paid for by the English."

"A knight, huh? What does the knight look like?"

"He is stout in frame, vicious and bloodthirsty, and he has one ear." He chuckled at the last.

"Isn't he famous for hating water? If that's true, he might stop chasing you once you set sail to Rum."

How would she know that? Iain and his friends knew of Thomas's fear of water, but they had known him since school. He doubted it was public knowledge. He regarded her and furrowed his brows. Did she know Thomas? Of all the strange things she had said, that was the most odd.

Iain kept his thoughts to himself and agreed. "Aye. We need to get to the nearest port and sail south to Rum. We'll skirt Inverness and go straight west over the mountains."

If they could gain passage, and if Cumberland's forces stayed to the roads, they could be ahead of them by days. He had to prepare his keep and his people.

CHAPTER 17

Three tortuous days passed before they finally made it to the mountains and found a cave to rest in. Abby didn't have to worry about keeping her distance from Iain during that time because he was staying as far from her as he could. She knew he had a lot on his mind— so did she—but other than keeping her warm at night, he hardly said a word.

She eyed the four-legged beast and screwed up her face. She didn't want to get back on the horse that morning. Her entire body was just too sore. "Can't we stay here for another day?" She didn't like the whine in her voice, but she couldn't help it.

Iain finished putting out the fire and made his way into the small cave they had spent the night in. As he passed Abby, he paused. "It's only been three days, Abigail."

"Three of the worst days of my life."

"I am sorry ye are in pain, but we have to keep moving."

Abby nearly snorted. He didn't sound sorry. Since the near kiss three days before, an invisible wall had gone up between them. He was colder and kept to himself most of the time.

They hardly talked, and even when they did, it was only because Abby asked questions of their surroundings and he had to answer or be overtly rude.

She eyed Iain saddling the horse and screwed up her face. They had bought the saddle from an old couple at a farmhouse, and while it was slightly more comfortable than bareback, it still hurt her back, butt, and thighs.

Abby stood up, moaning and rubbing her back. Iain never even glanced in her direction. The oaf was ignoring her. "I'll check to make sure we have everything," she said, and stomped into the cave.

By the time she exited the cave, Iain was ready and waiting. She let out a small huff and allowed him to help her onto the horse. The movement was getting easier with practice. Abby understood if she did a little jump at the same time Iain lifted, she didn't have to scramble so much and make the horse jittery. She quickly threw her leg over and waited for Iain to mount behind the saddle. She supposed she should be thankful. At least she had the saddle. The poor man had to sit on the horse's back behind, and that couldn't have been comfortable.

৩৯৩

ANOTHER WEEK PASSED, AND ABBY COULDN'T TAKE THE tension between them any longer. Yes, her body was getting used to the hours upon hours of riding. So much so, she was sure she had callouses on her butt. Either that or she had become accustomed to being numb and her body thought that was her normal. She guessed that was so, at least until she got home and could sit in comfy chairs and sleep on a real bed.

Stopping that night, Iain once again caught a rabbit that he roasted on a wet stick over a fire. Watching him pour water on the stick so it wouldn't burn had Abby smiling. She would have never thought to do that, and her chest warmed at his inventiveness.

After removing the rabbit, Iain handed her the full torso and munched down on the thighs and legs. She made a face, trying to make him take more, but as always, he said, "Eat. You need your strength. We still have a long way to go."

She tried to argue. "Fine, but what about you? You're bigger than me, and you're the one who hunts, looks after the horse, and cooks."

He gave her a wide smile, and little lines appeared at the corners of his eyes and mouth. Her heart skipped a beat. That was the smile she'd been hoping for since she'd met him.

"I believe ye are right," he said. "Ye can cook from now on."

Abby's mouth fell open, and she stared at her piece of rabbit.

He laughed. "Ye've been watching me since the first time I cooked that stew. Surely ye have learned something."

Thinking about the way he wet the roasting sticks, she screwed up her nose and said, "I suppose I have, and I suppose I can at least try, but you can't complain, all right?"

"That is fair. Now eat."

Abby did what she was told and tried to remember what he'd put in that stew. If she made enough, they would both have full stomachs.

After another long day's riding, they finally stopped near a small stream. The water was so clean, Abby could see the floor of small rocks on the bottom.

"It's beautiful," she said.

"Aye, and cold," Iain mumbled as he looked after the horse. He found a stick, and picking up each hoof, he cleaned it and gently placed it back on the ground. After he finished, he patted the horse on its rump and watched it walk to the water's edge. He seemed preoccupied as he and Abby collected some wood for a small fire.

"I won't be long."

He didn't need to say where he was going. Abby knew he was hoping to find another rabbit. She made a face. If she never saw another rabbit again, it would be too soon.

Before he disappeared into the brush, he turned and pierced her with his gaze. "Stay here and don't wander away. I won't be far."

"I know what to do," she said, staring hard back at him.

He chuckled and left.

She growled. "I'm not stupid, and he should know that by now." She stomped down to the water's edge. "Why does he always have to tell me what to do?"

She sucked in a breath. She knew why he was always telling her not to wander, to stay close to their camping area. He just wanted her to be safe, and she couldn't fault him for that. In fact, she had to admit that she quite liked it.

Dipping her hands in the freezing wet, she laughed as she splashed it on her face.

Refreshed and feeling alive once more, Abby spotted nettle growing a small distance away. She quickly filled the cooking pot they carried with them with water and placed it on the fire. Excited about finally making a stew, she made her way to the nettles and, using her skirt over her hands, picked a good-sized bunch.

In no time, she had the nettle broth simmering perfectly, and she sat back, waiting for Iain.

Iain returned, but his hands were empty. "I'm sorry. I couldn't find any rabbits."

He looked so forlorn, it was all Abby could do not to jump up and hug him. Instead, she looked at the simmering broth and then smiled up at him. "That's okay. We'll just have to have soup. Do you like nettle soup?"

He visibly relaxed. Did he think she was going to be angry at him for not bringing meat?

He plonked down beside her. "I love it."

More days passed. Sometimes they had rabbit, sometimes they had broth, and sometimes they had nothing.

The days weren't so bad, and the hours fled when they talked about their homes, although Abby got the impression Iain kept his stories lighthearted because he didn't want to share more with her. She, on the other hand, only spoke about the stuff that could happen in any time, no specifics, just generalizations. More than once, she caught Iain's wary look. He must have known she was keeping things from him, but thank goodness, he never said anything.

Sleeping next to Iain was another thing, though. It was getting harder every night to lie there and pretend to fall asleep. She was waking more and more, trying to snuggle in closer to him, not for the cold, but for the alien feelings his closeness sent thrumming through her body.

She knew she had to be careful, but she also knew she was getting to like the man far too much. He was generous when it came to food, insisting Abby take her fill. He was protective, not letting Abby stray too far away from him. He was kind, both to her when he thought she was tired, and to the horse when he stopped to let it drink and eat. Each time, he cleaned its hooves and checked its legs.

It seemed the last few nights, all she could think of was kissing him again, and she'd come close to doing just that before she caught herself leaning toward him whenever they stood close together.

Smashing her lips together, she shook the thought of his lips on hers out of her mind and focused on their surroundings.

Iain kept the horse moving to the base of the mountains. She gazed up at the peaks. Snow still clung to the top of the mountains, but Iain had said it was summer, so she guessed the snow would melt in time.

It was still cold where they were, but the sun shone more often. After a few hours, Abby spied another small stream.

"Look, water."

"Aye, we'll rest here for a bit."

Once the horse had its fill of water, Abby found a grassy edge where she could sit. She took off her shoes and dangled her feet in the stream. It was still freezing but not as bad as previously, and she kept them submerged until she became used to the temperature. She wriggled out of the cloak and, scooping up handfuls of water, washed her face. Her hair would have to wait until they got somewhere warmer.

Glancing behind her, she saw Iain was still tending to the horse. He appeared engrossed with its hooves, so she took off her vest and undid the buttons on her shirt. Without taking it off completely, she washed under her arms as best she could. Standing up to use her skirt to dry herself, she half turned and froze.

Iain was watching her with a peculiar expression on his face. Was his eyes narrowed in admiration or confusion? No matter how long she spent with him, she couldn't make out his moods.

"You stay there," Abby said, spinning back to face the stream.

"Aye."

She quickly dried herself and buttoned up her shirt. Once she'd put on the vest and cloak again, she turned around and came face to face with Iain.

"I am sorry the accommodations aren't more suitable for a woman such as yerself."

"They're fine." She ducked her head and moved to make her way around the tree.

Iain held her arm as she passed, and she stopped and

looked up at him expectantly. Those weird tingly feelings started zinging through her body again.

His gaze seemed to take in her whole face but settled on her lips.

Abby couldn't stop her body from leaning toward him if she tried, and she didn't bother trying. She knew he wanted to kiss her, and blast it all, she wanted to kiss him. Her eyes began to close, but he let her go.

"The horse is lame," he said.

"Lame?"

"Aye, it means he can't be ridden anymore."

Abby frowned. She was sure he wanted to kiss her, and she was even more sure she would have let him. "I know what lame means," she snapped.

Her bottom lip dropped, and she turned away so he wouldn't see her pout. Feeling a little silly at her reaction, Abby hurried to the fire Iain had built. She let the warmth soak into her cold skin and relaxed somewhat, but her mind wouldn't stop reminding her how much she'd wanted him to take her into his arms and kiss her. She also kept wondering why he hadn't taken the opportunity. Surely if he wanted to kiss her, that would have been the perfect time to do it. Maybe. Was she wrong? It wouldn't be the first time.

৩ֆֆ৩

Iain tarried with the horse while Abigail warmed herself by the fire. He glanced her way but took a second, longer look when he realized her eyes were shut. She was frowning, and he wondered what she was thinking . . . if she was thinking about how close they had come to kissing . . . again.

He shook his head. He had to control his actions around her all the time. He didn't know why he'd stopped her from walking past him, but just touching her arm had his mind whirling and all logical thought seemed to fly away. He had stepped forward, and without conscious thought, he'd intended to kiss her, but the snap of a branch under his boot pulled him back to reality.

He didn't know if he was thankful for that or not, but he had to acknowledge it was for the best. She would soon go back to her family, and he, too, would return to his family and responsibilities. He decided then and there, his first responsibility would be to tell Laird MacKinnon, he would not be marrying his daughter. Even if he couldn't have a future with Abigail, he knew he didn't want one with Fiona.

Abigail lifted her face to the sun. The sun shining on her bronze hair made Iain's chest tighten, and when she smiled at the sky, an ache he had never felt before shot through his heart.

He snapped his gaze from her to the horse. He had to find her treasure and return her to her family before he did something he couldn't undo.

When he thought she'd had enough time to rest, he tapped her on the shoulder. "Time to go."

She screwed up her nose at him but smiled and got to her feet.

He had no choice but to leave the horse, hoping someone would find it and nurse it back to health.

He decided they would have to make their way through the forest. It would be a harder walk, but safer than the roads. As they trudged up a slight rise, he hoped walking would exhaust him and he would finally be able to get some sleep that night.

He was finding it increasingly harder to stay away from the lass. She was not only beautiful, but she was stronger than she looked. Not too many lasses would have endured what she had since she'd met him, especially ones of high breeding.

She never complained. A grin spread over his face. Well, hardly ever, but that was in the beginning, and he understood it was only because her body ached with the abuse it had been subjected to as she rode the horse.

They were three days out of Rum, and a thought crossed Iain's mind that he could stray off course without the lass's knowledge. His family and clan had almost certainly given him up for dead by now. They would already be adjusting to a life without their laird.

He glanced at Abigail. He wanted to spend more time with her. He knew she was keeping secrets, and although he wanted nothing more in the world than to have her trust him enough to tell him such confidences, he had no right to demand she share them. After all, not only were they from two different worlds—him, a Highlander, and she a wealthy American—but they would soon part, him to go home and resume his duties as laird of his clan, and her, back to America.

No. He had to keep his distance, and the only way to do that was to get to Rum and send her to her family.

A shooting pain sliced through his heart at the thought of her boarding a coach and leaving him behind.

The crack of a branch snapping pulled him out of his reverie, and he glanced back.

How he hadn't noticed before that moment, he didn't know, but Abigail sounded like a herd of horses crashing through the undergrowth.

Iain stopped and whispered when she got close enough. "Ye must try to walk more softly. Look where ye place your feet and don't stand on dry sticks or branches."

Abigail narrowed her eyes and Iain thought she was going to argue with him, but she said, "Okay, then, I'll try."

Their pace had slowed somewhat, but having asked

Abigail to be careful, he couldn't possibly ask her to now hurry.

As they walked, Iain couldn't get visions of kissing her from his mind. His logical side knew he had to keep his distance. It was his duty as laird to strengthen his clan, and to that end, he must marry Fiona MacKinnon, but his heart, his body, wanted nothing more than to be with the strange girl clomping through the undergrowth, to hear her laugh.

He glanced back. She seemed to be concentrating on placing her feet. She was trying so hard to be quiet but also to keep up her pace. She didn't want to slow him down, and he smiled.

He suspected she was used to a lady's life and that she'd never traveled so hard for so long. But she was a fighter. He saw that in the way she tried to protect the MacDonald women, the way she wouldn't give up on him when he was feverish, the way she swallowed her fear and pain and rode the horse for as long as she did.

She was something special, and Iain needed to know more about her.

As soon as the path widened, he held back and walked beside her.

"Tell me more about yer family. Is it a hard life in America?"

"No, not hard, exactly, just different. We have nice houses, but we all work for them. There are no royals or gentry. We are all equal, um, some more equal than others, of course. And while the last election was close, we still have a male president."

"As it should be."

"What? Why?"

"Men are stronger. It is their place to protect, fight for their families, their clans." A picture of his ma came to mind, and he chuckled. "Of course, that is how it seems on the outside, but I know from experience it is not always the men who rule."

Abigail smiled. "Oh? How so?"

"Some women, like my mother, are too strong to be suppressed. My father not only loved my mother, but he listened to her counsel above all others."

"Your father sounds like he was a sensible man."

"Either sensible or henpecked."

Abigail stopped and peered at him. "Sensible," she said as if there were no argument.

Iain laughed. "Aye."

That night, Iain stretched out in their makeshift bed and gazed at the stars. It was a wonderous night, still cold enough that he once again risked a fire, but for some reason, the ground felt more comfortable, the stars were brighter, and the moon's glow shone on Abigail's locks whenever he chanced a glance her way.

The lass was also looking up at the sky. "It's so beautiful when it's not raining."

Iain ignored the lass's habit of complaining about the rain. "Aye. I haven't been to America, but I've traveled through Europe, and the further south I went, the sky seemed to drift higher. The stars here are so close, I sometimes think I can pluck them from the sky."

"I admit I find the life here hard, but I will miss it when I leave."

A jolt shot through him at her mention of leaving. He didn't want her to go. He wanted to stay with her as long as he could, to learn her ways, to understand her. The thought crossed his mind he could go to America. He silently snorted. No. In another time and another place, he might have had that choice, but his role was decided for him at the moment of his birth. He had to stay to lead and protect his clan.

Images of the keep, his sister, and his friends flitted across his mind, and he knew then he would never leave Scotland.

He sat up and looked at Abigail, still watching the night sky.

"Even had I the choice, I wouldna want to live anywhere else."

Her bottom lip dropped, parting her lips, and she let out a soft sigh.

That was Iain's undoing. He rolled over to his side and scooped her up in his arms, and before she had a chance to object, he brushed his lips over hers. She gasped in surprise, not fright. She didn't pull away.

He kept kissing her, and she wrapped her hands around his neck. His heart jumped into his throat at her acquiescence. The kiss was deep and long, and Iain had to fist his hands in her cloak to stop them from roaming where they shouldn't. He kept kissing her until a moan from deep in her throat sparked in his brain.

He knew then he could take her, but he also knew he couldn't let his base emotions rule him. He was a ruler; he was stronger than that. She pulled back, but only far enough to nibble at his bottom lip. Another moan sounded, but this time, it was from deep within his chest, and he held her tighter.

She gazed up into his eyes.

Heated passion whirled in her stormy eyes, and he answered, bending his head to kiss her again, but hesitated. She wriggled closer to him, giving him consent to continue, yet although he wanted her physically, he realized at that moment, if he continued, he would never let her go. He would follow her to the ends of the earth just to taste her full pink lips. He wanted more. He wanted her heart, her soul, her everything. But he couldn't have any of those things without knowing what secrets she harbored.

He let her go and stood up.

Staring down at her large confused eyes, he said, "We have to talk."

She closed her eyes and bit her lip. "Now?"

As Iain persuaded the fire to intensify, Abigail drew her cloak and the blankets around her shoulders.

She gazed into the fire. "So, what do you want to talk about?"

"We cannae have a relationship with secrets between us."

She snapped her head up and stared at him. "A relationship?"

Iain balked. Had he misread her emotions? Had she just wanted a physical dalliance? Didnae she want a relationship with him?

He couldn't say anything. He just stared into the fire, wondering how he could have gotten everything so wrong.

Perching on a rock close to his legs, Abigail pulled down on his kilt. "Sit down."

Like a man possessed of little brain, he did so, but he didn't take his eyes off the dancing flames.

Abigail let out a long, loud breath. "I do have a secret, Iain, but I don't know if you are strong enough to hear it."

His back stiffened, and he glared at her. How dare she question his strength, his manhood?

"Don't get weird on me. I meant the secret is something so, um, out of this world, I doubt anyone in Scotland at this time would be able to handle it." Her eyes widened. "Hang on, you said we both have secrets. You tell me yours first, and I just might tell you mine."

Still trying to make out what she said in the first instance, Iain raised his eyebrows. "What do ye mean by 'Scotland at this time'?"

"Don't change the subject." She smiled. "What's your secret?"

Her perfect smile shot straight to his heart, and he knew if she was to leave him, his heart would never feel that way again. He had to tell her the truth and hope she wouldn't think less of him.

"I am to wed."

She reared back. "What? You're engaged and yet you still kissed me, tried to make out with me?"

"Make out what?"

"Never mind, but you did kiss me. More than once, I might add."

Iain hanged his head unable to meet her angry eyes. She was right, he was a cad. "I am not affianced, but I am expected to wed the daughter of our neighboring clan, the MacKinnons."

CHAPTER 18

A bby didn't want him to regret kissing her, but she knew he was right; there was no way they could be together. She studied his lowered profile, his jaw was set hard and his lips were tight and thin. He couldn't look unhappier with his situation.

"Don't you like your girlfriend?"

"Girlfriend? I have many friends, both young and old lasses."

"The girl you're supposed to marry."

"She is beautiful."

Abby had to stop herself from wincing at that proclamation.

"And she is a highborn Scot."

Of course, she was. Another strike against Abby.

"Then what's the problem?"

He looked at her, hurt and disappointment in his eyes. "I dinnae love her."

"Oh."

What else could she say? Arranged marriages were the norm in Iain's time, and she was sure they couldn't back out of one once they were announced. It was probably for the best. She had to go home, and he had to get married . . . To someone else. She gnawed at her bottom lip.

"Well, I'm sure you will learn to love her once you get to know her."

"I already know her. She is young and braw, aye, but has a mean streak I dinnae think I can live with." He slapped his knees and stood up. "I willna marry Fiona."

Elation coursed through Abigail but she immediately grimaced. What was she thinking? He needed to continue with his life the way he was doing before he met her.

She swallowed, hoping she wasn't the cause for his change of heart. "Did you just come to that decision right now?"

"Nay, I've been thinking on it for some time. Fiona would be as miserable with me as I would be with her. It isna right to make people marry."

"What about her father?"

Iain let out a sigh. "Laird MacKinnon might have a different point of view, but mayhap we can come to an arrangement."

Abby frowned. Wars were fought for much less in these times. Clans were always squabbling with one another over land, animals, and whatever else they could come up with. She smiled again. "I hope things will work out for you."

"Aye, now tell me yer secret." He squatted in front of her, piercing her with his gaze. "Where are ye really from? And tell me about the strange fashion ye were wearing when ye rescued me."

It was Abby's turn to stand up. She moved closer to the dwindling fire and stared into the flames. How was she to tell him the truth? He wouldn't believe her. It would be too much for him.

"You won't believe me," she said.

He stood up beside her. "I'll know if yer not telling the truth."

Wringing her hands, Abby swallowed, but her mouth had gone dry. Maybe she could come up with a better story. No, she had to tell him the truth. He already knew she was too different from her choice of words, and he'd seen her modern clothes, though, at the time, she'd hoped he was too sick to notice.

"I think you'd better sit down again before I tell you."

He regarded her for a moment and, with a shrug, sat down on the rock. He regally waved his hand as if showing her a room at an open house. "Ye have my attention, lass."

She gave him a wry look and sighed. "You're not going to believe me, but what I'm going to tell you is the truth."

Rubbing her sweaty palms on her skirt, she tried to find the right way of telling him something that was still bizarre to her, let alone what it would be to him. She widened her arms to show him her clothes. "You've noticed this isn't my normal style of dress. The ones I was wearing when you woke up in that first cabin were my real clothes."

He nodded. Something lit his gaze as his eyes roamed from her head to her feet and back again. Was it admiration?

"I know you didn't approve of my attire, but where I come from, it is quite tame, really. Professional, even."

"Where do ye come from?" He snorted. "Even I know women in the Americas dinnae dress like that. They are as modest, more so even, than the lasses here."

"Look, just open your mind, will you?" She rubbed her face and, letting her arms drop, she decided to just come out with it. "I am not from here. I'm not supposed to be here. I'm supposed to be in another time." She stopped and looked directly into his eyes. "I am from the future."

"The future?" He doubled over laughing.

"Don't laugh at me, buster. You wanted the truth and that's what I'm telling you so you could at least listen."

His brows shot up then drew together in a scowl, but humor still sparked in his dark eyes.

"Trust me. If I could, I'd go back right now, but I can't." She massaged her temples. "That Thomas jerk has my time device."

He jumped up and clasped her forearm, his eyes widened in confusion. "Ye expect me to believe ye are no' of this world?"

"I . . ." She stepped back. "You're hurting me."

He gawked at his hand and dropped her arm.

"My apologies." His jaw tightened, and his eyes narrowed, piercing her with his gaze. "Thomas has yer *ti-ime* device?"

She knew instantly he didn't believe her.

His eyes were hard and cold. Judging her. If she was any good at reading body language, he had just labeled her mad.

She sighed. "Yes, and you said you'd help me get it back."

Turning abruptly, Iain strode into the dark. Abby stayed rooted to the spot, staring at his back. He tipped his head back and raised his arms above his head as if he was beseeching God for something.

He stayed like that for a long moment, spun on his heels and returned to the light of the fire.

"I am obliged to listen to more of yer story. After all, ye being there at the exact time I needed help must have been God's doing. For that, I thank God."

"I'm good with that." Abby sometimes wished she could have that sort of faith in a heavenly being. She had often thought it would make life easier, but then she would wonder if all the carrying on about sins would fill her with guilt. What she saw as everyday feelings and actions, the religious thought sinful. One came to mind immediately. Having sex before marriage. She bit the inside of her cheek. Maybe she should have followed that edict.

She had been intimate with her last boyfriend, and after he ran off, she'd wished she hadn't given Peter that part of herself. If she was honest, it wasn't as earth-shatteringly amazing as she'd thought it would be.

She glanced at Iain. People of his time expected the women they married to be virgins. She gave a silent snort. Of course, no one expected the men to be virginal.

IAIN SPOKE LITTLE TO ABIGAIL THAT NIGHT. HE WAS thankful she hadn't tried to convince him what she said was the truth and instead left him to think about her proclamation. He couldn't believe she was from the future, of course. How could she be? But he could believe she was confused or mayhap she'd had a head injury, and mayhap she'd lost her memory. If she did not know who she was or where she came from that would explain her befuddlement, and seeing how different she was from the Scots, she'd conceived she was not of their time.

As he drifted to sleep, his father's strange friends came to mind. At six years of age, he could tell they were different. It occurred to him in that fuzzy time before sleep took him, they could have been related to Abigail. She was similar in appearance to the man. With her oblong face, her straight nose and narrow nostrils, and pointed chin. Although her eyes were blue-gray like his father's female friend.

He decided to ask her about them, but still couldn't remember their names.

The next morning, Iain got up before Abigail and was just about to restart the fire when muffled voices sounded on the other side of a small hill. He ducked and scrambled to Abigail, shaking her to awaken her.

She moaned, and Iain quickly put his hand over her mouth. Her eyes snapped open. "Shh," he whispered, and pointed to the hill. "Someone is on the other side of that knoll."

Abigail nodded, and he let his hand go. He nodded to the boulders they huddled beside. "Hide behind there."

Abigail scooped up the bedding and scampered behind the rocks, and Iain crept up the hill, dropping to his stomach just before he reached the top and peeking over the rise.

Thomas, with a bandaged head, followed the road west. Three English soldiers rode to his rear.

Iain smiled. Only four. He could handle them. Once they were around the bend, Iain quietly followed but kept to the side of the road. The road forked ahead, and Iain was delighted they turned to the left fork that led to Uram.

Abigail's confession sparked in his mind. He would retrieve her treasure as he had promised, but then they would part company, she to Inverness and her family, and once he found a boat, he would sail to Rum.

CHAPTER 19

Two weeks and two days since they'd left the farmhouse, Iain and Abby walked into the port town of Uram. Abby straightened, stretching the tight ligaments in her back. She was relieved to finally stop traveling and ecstatic at the thought of getting the orb back from Sir Thomas. Her shoulders slumped. Once she had the orb, she would go home. She was already beginning to miss Iain and the time they had spent together.

Abby had never in her life wanted a man as much as she wanted her Highlander. He was gentle and caring, and although Abby hated traveling across the country, she loved being close to Iain.

She glanced back over her shoulder. Iain was stone-faced. He didn't believe her explanation about time travel, and she hoped he wasn't about to change his mind about getting the orb back for her.

"We need a boat and supplies before we find Thomas," Iain said. "A stable boy will know what's about."

At the inn, he stopped and pulled her close into his side. "Stay by me," he said.

She turned her face up to his and was immediately drawn into his dark gaze. His lips touched her hair as she leaned into him. His head bent forward, and sure he was finally going to kiss her, Abby tipped her head back and closed her eyes.

He let out what Abby could only comprehend as an impatient sigh, and quickly moved away, but clasped her hand in his. Abby snapped her eyes open. She felt like a fool . . . an *eejit*, as the Scots would say. She blinked back tears as she stood there, not knowing what to do or say. It confused her, but soon, anger bubbled up through her, and she bundled the blanket of belongings close to her chest to keep a barrier between them.

Iain handed some coins to the young stable hand. "Where can we get supplies?"

"There be a store 'alfway 'tween 'ere and the port, m'lord." His eyes flashed with recognition and he whispered, "M'lord, the army is 'ere in search of Jacobites."

Iain nodded and kept his voice low. "Where?"

"They're going from door to door, sir. Searching all the alleyways and warehouses. They've searched here already and was on the other side of the dock last I heard."

Iain's brows furrowed more.

"Thank you," Abby said, smiling at the boy.

Color shaded his freckled cheeks as he bowed. "Thank ye, m'lady."

Iain guided Abby along the buildings. He chuckled. "I think ye have another admirer, m'lady."

Abby smiled. "*Another* one? I never knew I had any."

"Aye, ye do."

She cocked her head and raised her brows. "You?"

"Aye. Now no more talk. We need to gather supplies."

He had tried to sound lighthearted, but Abby winced at the worry tingeing every word. Oh, she understood he wanted to confront Thomas on his own terms. That was why his eyes often darted from side to side, peering into the distance, and scowling as if he could smell the soldiers. He confused her by all but saying outright he admired her when at other times, he snubbed her to the point of bringing her close to tears.

She hoped they could get the time device from Thomas. Then once she'd disappeared before his very eyes, he would have to believe her. Of course, that wouldn't do her any good. She'd be home with her brother and sisters, probably pining away for her Highlander until she died.

Abby gazed at his profile. His lips were drawn tight, and his jaw twitched. He still had her hand in his, but the warmth had dissipated. There was a cold fury emanating out of his very pores. He yanked on her hand, nearly pulling her arm out of its socket, and whisked her and himself around the side of the inn.

His hard eyes alighted on her upturned face. He scowled a warning to be quiet.

He didn't need to caution her. She wasn't stupid.

Was he regretting having to drag her around with him and regretting his promise to get her treasure? She was slowing him down; she knew that.

Three soldiers marching shoulder to shoulder stomped down the road. Two more followed in their wake.

Abby stayed perfectly still and held her breath until no more heavy boots sounded.

Iain tugged her to go, but she held back. "Maybe you should go ahead without me?"

Hot fury flashed in his eyes, and then they filled with what Abby could only guess was fear.

"Nay."

Fear? Of course, he would fear the English.

He tugged her hand. "Ye wouldna last an hour here on ye own."

Together, they skulked down the street close to the buildings. The sun was setting, and shadows had Abby jumping so often, Iain must have thought she was being bitten by something.

Someone shouted behind them, "Laird Iain MacLaren."

Iain snapped his head back. "Damn."

Pulling Abby with him, he set off at a run. Guns fired. He and Abby ducked and scampered around a building, not stopping until they had traversed the smelly and muddy dirt—at least, Abby hoped it was mud—to the other side of the building. Iain stretched his neck and looked around the corner.

Abby bent under his arm and looked too.

Sir Thomas Sutherland stalled at the alleyway. "I know you are there, MacLaren. Go get him, men."

His men surged forward and out of sight.

Iain guided Abby back down the road and rounded another corner into the main thoroughfare. Wagons, horses, and people were hurrying in all directions. Some arriving, some leaving, some going home to their dinners and family, and some making their way to inns.

Abby was glad to see the road so busy. Surely Thomas wouldn't risk firing guns in the crowd.

Iain and Abby moved into a group of loud ruffians, trying to lose themselves in the throng.

Finally, Iain shoved his way through the door of a store, dragging her behind him. "Act naturally," he whispered. "Ye don't know who ye can trust."

He plucked fresh bread from the baskets and plopped them on the counter and grated out the rest of his list. "Two pounds of dried meat and one pound of cheese."

The bell above the door sounded, and Abby glanced up. Thomas and two soldiers stood there. Thomas laughed, his eyes sinister and bloodthirsty.

Before Abby could react, Iain threw a bread basket at

Thomas's face with one hand, drew his sword with the other, and lunged forward. Thomas sidestepped but soon regained his balance and leapt out of the way. Iain fought the two soldiers, baskets and shelves falling in their wake. The storekeeper kept shouting, "Nay. Ma store. Ma store."

Thomas was edging around behind Iain. Abby threw her hand over her mouth. The bastard was going to attack from behind. Coward. Abby snapped her head around, looking for a weapon, anything that would stop Thomas's advance.

She grabbed a poker that was leaning against some shelving and crept forward. Thomas lifted his sword high, and as his shoulder twitched to bring the blade down, Abby whopped him over the head with the poker.

He cried out and spun around on his shaky heels. His face raged red, and he brought his sword around, ready to lop off Abby's head, but stayed his hand at the last moment. His beady eyes ogled Abigail's torn shirt.

Abby knew she should have hit him harder, but at the last minute, she had instinctively reduced the impact. Stupid. She was in a kill-or-be-killed situation, and she didn't knock the creep out? If she were there, Max would be furious with her.

Thomas turned back to the fight, and Abby's gaze caught the top of a white object poking out of his pants pocket. Her orb. Abby glanced up. Iain had felled one soldier, but the other one had him up against the wall.

"Kill him, soldier," Thomas demanded. "This on—"

Before he'd finished talking, not making the same mistake again, Abby swung the poker through the air and landed it full force against his left shoulder.

Darn.

She had aimed for his head.

Thomas side-skipped into a great bag leaning on the wall. The jars above tottered and then fell off the shelf. Glass and honey shattered over his dirty coiffured wig. His eyes were open but glazed. Abby took her chance. She plucked the orb out of his pocket. "This is mine, you jerk."

Iain used the snag in his opponent's concentration to haul a heavy rope Abby recognized as a ship's hawser around the soldier's neck and disarm him.

Abby scooted past Thomas and into Iain's arms.

"Is that your treasure?" he asked, nodding to her orb.

"Yes," she said, and grinned.

Not having time to explain any further, Abby took Iain's hand, and they fled the store where more soldiers waited for their commander. With her nails biting into Iain's hand, Abby kept her hold on the orb as if she would die if she were to lose it again.

Thomas must have gotten his wits back, because his voice bawled out behind them, "Get them!"

Boots pounded the dirt road, and guns fired. Iain and Abby dodged and swerved, swerved and dodged, yelling all the while for people to take cover just as a horse's clomping hoofbeats echoed in the air around them.

"Sir Thomas, Sir Thomas!" someone shouted.

"What?" Thomas's voice bellowed over the top of the gunshots.

The first voice answered, but Abby couldn't make out his words above the sound of the muskets, and her thundering heart. Thomas couldn't have either, because he yelled for his men to halt.

Iain wasn't going to let the chance go by. He yanked Abby closer to his side, and they skidded around the corner at the end of the street.

They stopped and listened. No bootsteps followed them. Abby panted, taking great gulps of air into her burning lungs.

"What?" Thomas again.

"An order, sir." The first voice.

Silence ensued and Abby got her breaths under control, but her heart was still dancing a jig against her ribcage.

"I can't read it in this light," Thomas said. "What does it say?"

"Lord Cumberland has ordered your regiment to France."

"When?"

"Immediately, sir. It seems he thinks you are in Aberdeen and tells you to wait for him there."

Abby's heart leapt, and she smirked at the string of curses issuing from Thomas's lips.

Iain hugged her and whispered, "We are to be safe."

"Find MacLaren now!" Thomas hollered, and the sounds of stomping boots heading in their direction filled the street.

"Quickly," Iain said, tugging at Abby's hand.

Abby faltered.

"Faster," Iain said, nearly pulling her feet off the ground.

She gritted her teeth and dug her nails harder into his flesh, and bringing her feet in line with her body, she coursed beside him along the dock. A large rowboat bobbed behind a large ship. Iain untied the rope from the dock and threw it into the boat. "Jump," he shouted into Abby's ear.

A bullet whizzed by them. Abby glanced back at their pursuers, and with adrenaline screaming at her to take flight, she leapt into the boat. Iain landed less than a second later and both their bodies crashed to the floor of the boat. Musket bullets sang over their heads and splashed into the water behind them.

Iain scrambled up, grabbed the oars, and began rowing. "Keep down."

Abby did as she was told as Thomas shouted threats and curses.

Her eyes widened in realization that she was now an outlaw. She held the orb. Should she take Iain and disappear into time? What would he do? How would he react to her modern time? She didn't care; she had to save him. She put her hand over the top of the orb and tensed her fingers, ready to twist the top so the leaves aligned. She was sure that was what she'd done at home, but she stilled. What if the orb didn't take her home? What if the stupid thing took her to an entirely different time and place? Should she risk it?

"We're out of range," Iain said, his shoulders slumping with exhaustion.

Warily, Abby raised her head and looked back to the dock. Little plops in the water told her the bullets couldn't make the distance to the boat—to them. She clutched the orb to her chest and fell, exhausted, back onto the boat floor. Her head swirled with dire thoughts of traveling to different times, but she knew she'd have to use the orb sooner or later. She decided that later was her best option for the time being.

CHAPTER 20

I ain continued to plough the oars through the water. Although Thomas had stopped pursuing them, Iain couldn't be sure other enemies wouldn't follow. They had to get south before anyone could capture or kill them.

A smile twitched the corners of his mouth. If Thomas could see himself, he'd realize he had no reason to be furious at Iain. His half ear improved his looks immensely and made him appear formidable. Surely, he could gain some recognition in the French court and mayhap some warm sympathy from the court lasses.

Abigail sat up and asked, "Are you all right?"

He bent and kissed the top of her head.

Her brows drew together, and her eyes clouded with confusion. Mayhap she thought he had been shot.

"Aye, I am well. None of the bullets came near to hitting either of us." He smiled, trying to allay her fears. "If ye are right and Sir Thomas dislikes traveling on water, he is not going to like sailing to France."

"Good. I hope he gets sea sickness and heaves his stomach up all the way."

Ian laughed. "Aye. The very thought warms my heart." He set about rhythmically rowing. "We should get to Rum in a few days."

She turned her head, and fire lit Iain's veins as she kissed his chin. Her lips rested there, and he felt her warm breath from her sigh. "Thank you."

"Sleep now," he said. "We have a ways to go."

"What about you?"

"I will rest on the morrow. Tonight, I want to go some distance."

Abigail scrunched the roll of blankets under her head and gazed at him. The deep blue of the ocean reflected in her eyes pulling him under. He admired her luscious lips. As if Abigail could read his mind, she opened her mouth in a small smile.

The smooth motion of his rowing faltered but with a huge effort, he regained his rhythm. Did she not know how besotted he was?

Trying to moisten his dry mouth, he swallowed. "If ye don't stop looking at me like that, we willnae be going anywhere."

She lifted her chin and shot him a mischievous grin. "Sorry."

"Liar."

She laughed and turned her head away.

How he loved that sound. Music floating on water. He frowned. He had to protect her, and he would, with his very life if he had to.

They both must have been high on adrenaline, because their happiness at their safe escape wiped out any of the tension that had grown between them since she told him her secret.

Iain still didn't believe her, but a question had grown in his mind sending his thoughts into a whirl. His father's friends were fun people to a six-year-old. He had to get

Abigail to agree to go to Dorpol with him. He wanted to show her the game they had made for him. Mark had called it a board game and it was nothing like any of the games he or his friends had seen before.

Iain peered into the dark and concentrated on keeping a constant rhythm to his rowing.

He glanced down. The moonlight lit the white of something in her hands. When she'd said her treasure was a time-traveling device, he'd never sensed a lie. She had insisted she never hit her head, but she wouldn't know that though if she'd lost her memory and imagined her arrival in Scotland via time instead of sailing over the sea from America.

"Abigail?"

She peered at him. "Yes?"

"Why haven't ye used that?"

She held up her keepsake and grimaced. "To tell you the truth, I think I know what I did to make me come back in time; it's just I'm not sure if the same thing will take me back home, to my time. I'm a bit scared I might end up some place else." She smiled, the moonlight catching on her teeth. "I know I have to try, but I'm a little scared."

He nodded and kept rowing. Eyeing her treasure, he frowned. If it was indeed a time device, surely, she could vanish now that she had it in her hands.

But what if she was telling the truth? He pushed down the pain of the thought. He couldn't lose her now. Now that he had met her, how would he live without her?

As he rowed, his mind kept alternating between believing time travel was possible and thinking himself mad for even considering such a thing.

Some hours later, Iain didn't know how many, his arms refused to move the oars. Using the last of his strength, he turned the boat into shore and as it bumped against the bank, he jumped out. He tied the rope to a tree a small way from the water and returned to the boat, nestling behind her, framing his form along hers.

She leaned back into him and moaned.

His body, now alert, had him nibbling her neck. He couldn't help it; he couldn't stay away from her.

She rolled over and her eyes fluttered open. She smiled. "Hi."

He grinned, but as he raised his arm over her shoulder, he grimaced. Every muscle in his arms cried out in agony with each movement. "Shh, go back to sleep."

She snuggled into his chest and sighed.

The next morning, Iain awoke with a start. It took him a moment to get his bearings, and when he remembered their predicament, he went through the actions to set them back away from shore.

Stretching and groaning, Abigail awakened. "Ooh, my muscles are so sore."

"Aye. It will be good to sleep in a bed once more."

"You're not joking there."

Iain chuckled. She had a strange language, but even if he didn't know what she said most of the time, he still loved the sound of her voice.

She sat up and looked at the sky.

"It's going to rain, isn't it?" She faced him, and her luscious lips formed a pout. "It's going to be miserable, isn't it?"

He laughed. Wherever she came from, rain must have been scarce. "Aye. But we can collect clean water in that bowl there." He pointed under the back bow.

Abigail picked up the pot and turned it over, gazing at it. She stared into it. "I don't want to know what it was used for before."

"I think it was used for cleaning fish."

"I said I didn't want to know." She sniffed the pot. "Well, at least whoever had it cleaned it."

Placing the pot on the floor between her seat and the bow, she said, "You don't look so hot."

"I am no' hot. I am a little tired, though."

She leaned forward and placed her palm on his forehead. "You're right, you don't have a fever, but you can't be sitting out here in the rain and cold."

"We don't have a choice. We have to get to Rum."

The rain fell lightly but never stopped the whole day and night. It was a continuous exasperating drizzle. Sometimes it was so light, Iain thought it had stopped altogether, and at other times, enough fell that they were both soaked to the skin.

He used his plaid to keep as much water off Abigail as possible during the night, but during the day, he thought it better to wear the thing, just in case they were spotted by someone from the shore.

By the third morning, Iain spotted Rum appear and disappear through the gray mist rising from the ocean on the horizon.

Abigail awoke coughing. Iain bent to feel her forehead before she could get to his brow. She wasn't feverish. "Ye are unwell."

"Nah." She smiled and swatted his hand away. "It's just a bit of a cold, that's all. I'll be right as soon as I'm dry, warm, and fed." She gazed at the wet dressing. "I can't change that out here."

Iain shrugged. "The wound is healed enough that a wet bandage won't hurt it." He nodded his head to his left. "Look there. Do ye see?"

Abigail gasped. "I see it."

He wished he could kiss the droplets of water off her nose, her eyes, her lips. No. He had to stop thinking that way. Once he sent word to her grandparents, she would leave. And although Iain didn't want to think she would board a boat and sail away, he knew in his heart, if not his head, that she had told him the truth. She didn't belong in his world. She was out of time, and once she remembered how to work that device, she would disappear from his life, from his time.

A thought struck him then. Once she returned to the future, he would have been long dead and buried. Would she grieve him?

He let out a long, slow breath. It was all much too complicated. He pulled the oars toward him.

She sat on the seat opposite Iain. "Let me row for a while?"

Iain shook his head.

"Stop being such a stubborn goat and let me row. Your arms must be killing you."

As if making their agreement with her known, the muscles in his arms cramped. He groaned. "Aye."

They swapped seats, and Abigail pulled the oars slowly through the water. Iain rubbed and then shook his lead-filled arms to try to bring life back to them. They would not get to Rum until nightfall if she rowed the whole way.

As if she'd read his mind, Abigail tilted her head and shook it. "Fine. I'll row for half an hour, and then you can take over again. Okay?"

"Okaay."

They both laughed, and Iain followed her eyes to her orb. He swallowed hard, needing to dislodge the pain in his chest, and gazed at the island growing before them. He reveled in the thought that Abigail would soon be in his home. His keep wasn't as grand as some, but it was comfortable, and his people were happy.

After about half an hour, Iain peered at their destination. His island only appeared slightly closer.

He held out his hands. "I'll take over now."

They swapped places, and Abigail shook out her hands in much the same way as Iain had earlier.

The orb in her lap taunted him over his thoughts, and again, the idea of her disappearing from his life for all time had a brick growing in his chest, making it hard to breathe.

His jaw hardened. He kept rowing, kept getting nearer to their destination. He refused to think about losing his lifeblood, the angel of his heart. *Oh, God. Why did you send her to me only to take her away again? Why? Why?*

CHAPTER 21

Abby wiped her wet face with her even wetter skirt as Iain moored the boat. Once her feet found solid ground, she didn't know if her legs still thought they were at sea or if it was the three riders galloping toward them that made her legs shake. She stumbled forward, but Iain caught her up before she fell face-first into the wet mud . . . again. He held her under his arm and waited for the riders to slow and then stop.

A great red-haired thing spoke in Gaelic and laughed loudly as he leapt to the ground.

Abby couldn't work out where his beard finished, and is hair began as both sets of locks entwined in the wind.

Iain and Big Red clasped their forearms, pulling each other close in a manly embrace. Iain also spoke in Gaelic, so Abby had no idea what was being said.

Iain looked at the other two brutes, one with brown hair and a short beard and a younger one, clean shaven, with light-brown hair, and nodded.

The smooth-faced man said something while Short Beard looked Abby over from head to foot.

She squirmed under his gaze, stepping in closer to Iain.

"Do not worry yer heart over Callum. He can't keep his eyes off a beautiful lass."

Short Beard slid from his horse and clasped Iain's arm in another forearm shake. Whatever he said had the other two bending over in laughter. He had obviously made a joke about her.

Abby straightened her back and, looking down her nose, cast her eyes over his form. She would ask Iain what the joke was later.

"Speak English," Iain said.

All three men turned their curious eyes to Iain. "Who is she?" the red-haired giant asked.

Iain gave her a one-armed hug. "She's my angel. She saved me from certain death on the Culloden battlefield."

He pointed to the red-haired brute. "This be Donal and" —he nodded to Short Beard—"Callum, and the young lad there is Alistair."

"Ah, I think a story is to be heard this night," Donal said. "Maeve will be beside herself when she finds you have returned. Alistair, go tell Maeve Iain has returned to us."

The clean-shaven young man grinned. "Aye," he shouted and turning his horse, he kicked it into a canter He disappeared over a rise, his long brown hair trailing after him.

Donal waved his arm at Callum then jabbed his thumb in the air behind his back. Callum leapt from his horse, gave the reins to Iain, and jumped behind Donal.

"We'll ready the keep," Donal said, kicking his horse into a gallop back the same way they had come.

Abby stared after them. "They work for you?"

"Aye, though 'work with me' would be a better way to say it. They are brave and honest men. The best of the MacLaren clan."

Abby could see by the look of pride on his face how much the men meant to him.

Iain placed his hands around her waist and plopped her onto the front of the saddle before mounting behind her. He drew her in close to his chest. "You are safe here, lass."

She turned and smiled. She hadn't meant for her worries to show on her face.

The gate had already been lowered by the time they arrived at the castle. A woman stood on the stairs, and the moment she spotted Iain, she began running toward him.

"Iain. Iain." The bun at the back of her neck bounced haphazardly as she ran, bunching her skirt up high in front of her.

She wore the MacLaren tartan colors on her shawl. Something attached to her lower leg glinted in the sun that poked through dark clouds. Abby squinted. It was a knife. Did even the women arm themselves? Iain had said she was safe here, but if she had to wear weapons attached to her body, that didn't bode well.

"That," Iain said, admiration filling his voice. "Is my sister."

He leapt from behind the saddle. Maeve rushed into his arms. "Yer home! I have missed ye."

"And I ye, Sister." He swooped her up and spun her small frame around. Her legs flew out behind her.

His sister looked the size of a child in Iain's arms. And she laughed like one too.

Maeve was still giggling when Iain brought her to a standing stop. She leaned back and eyed Abby. Iain let his sister go and lifted Abby off the horse.

"This is my sister, Maeve."

Abby smiled at the slight woman but remembering her manners and the time she was in, she gave a slight curtsy.

With his mouth twitching and his eyes full of humor, Iain

gave Abby's hand a squeeze.

"I am proud to introduce Abigail. She is my angel sent to me from God when I was all but done on the battlefield."

"You saved my brother?"

Abby glanced down and smoothed her skirt. A chunk of dry mud fell off.

"Aye, she did, and she has seen me healthy enough to return to ye."

Maeve eyed Abby. "I thank ye, then."

Abby smiled but couldn't help but think Maeve wasn't too pleased that Iain brought a woman to the castle.

Maeve linked her arm into Iain's elbow and started up the stairs. "We are already preparing for noontime, but now we shall have a feast tonight. Oh, and"—she gazed up at Iain but threw a quick glance at Abby—"the MacKinnons will be here this evening." She sniffed and glanced back at Abby. "But first, both of ye will bathe, eat, and rest."

By the time Maeve showed Abby to her room, a tub was already set before the fire.

"Ye don't talk much, do ye?" Maeve said, regarding Abby with a wary glance.

Abby had hoped the girl would just leave her be. She knew Maeve would question her speech, and there was no way she would try to sound Scottish. She was never any good at accents. Max was the one for that. She had a perfect ear for accents. "No, well, um, maybe you should talk to your brother about that."

"Yer speech is strange."

"It might seem so to you, but where I come from, it's pretty average."

"Where are ye from?"

"America, ah, the Americas."

Recognition piqued in Maeve's sky-blue eyes. "Och, aye. Many Scots are sailing there now."

"I've met some." Abby wasn't lying; she had met lots of Scots in her travels. She glanced longingly at the tub of steaming water.

"Och, I am sorry. I'll leave ye to yer bath and go and annoy my brother. Jannet will be along shortly."

"Jannet?"

"Ay, the maid."

The moment Maeve closed the door, Abby ripped off the filthy clothes she wore and sank into the heavenly water. She began scrubbing herself with the fragrant soap and hurriedly washed her hair. She wanted to be finished before the maid arrived. She knew in this time, they had servants, and while she liked the idea of someone other than her cooking and cleaning, she didn't need anyone to help her bathe. She smiled at the memory of her last day at a spa. A massage would be a win, though.

As she began rinsing out her hair, the door opened. She stopped and looked out from under her soapy strands.

A middle-aged woman carrying two buckets of water tisked. "Och, you'll never get the soap out of your hair that way." She placed the buckets at her feet and knelt beside the tub. "Get on your knees and bend your head as far forward as you can. And shut your eyes."

The woman gave orders like she was in the army. Max would have loved her. She pushed Abby's head down a bit more, and Abby had to hold the sides of the tub to stop from falling forward completely.

"I'm Jannet," the woman said as she picked up a bucket and poured some of the lukewarm water over Abby's head. She squeezed out the excess water and poured more, repeating the actions until she was satisfied. "There," she said, pouring the last of the water over Abby's head before once again squeezing the excess wetness out. She got to her feet and stood there as if waiting for something.

Abby flipped her hair back and gazed up at the woman. She was a stout woman with a straight back, but her face held warmth and, Abby thought, curiosity.

"Well, stand up."

"Huh? Can't you just hand me a towel?"

"Nay. I need to rinse ye off first."

Letting out a sigh, Abby stood up. This was just terrific. *Welcome to the eighteenth century, Abs.* It took all her control not to cover herself in front of the woman as Jannet poured the other bucket over her front, indicated she turn around, and then poured the rest of the water over her back.

"Oot now."

The moment Abby's second foot hit the floor, Jannet wrapped her in a robe. "Go sit by the fire, and I'll brush out yer hair."

Abby enjoyed Jannet brushing her hair. It was much more relaxing than having it blow-dried. More than once, her eyes closed of their own accord. Of course, she was tired, exhausted more like, but she thought even if she wasn't, she would find it difficult to keep awake during such ministrations.

A soft knock at the door sounded.

Jannet left Abby and answered. "Thank ye." She closed the door and put a tray on the small table pushed into the corner of the room.

With her hair nearly dry from the thorough brushing, Abby wearily sat at the table. A bowl of broth, a chunk of bread, and some cheese had her stomach rumbling. After nothing but water for days, she could hardly contain herself from attacking the tray. The smell of the beef broth rose to her nose, and she sighed.

"Eat up and rest. I will return to dress ye before the feast."

The moment Jannet left, Abby stuffed broth-sodden

bread into her mouth and ate her fill. She drained a mug of sweet mead before collapsing on the bed, wrapping herself in the downy cover, and immediately falling asleep.

What seemed like less than a minute later, Jannet roused her. "Time to get out of bed. The feast is already underway."

Abby refused to open her eyes. "Go away. I was dreaming."

"Och. Get up. I have to dress ye." And with that, the rotten maid threw the covers off, and goose pimples erupted all over Abby's naked body. It took her a moment to remember she had taken off the damp robe the woman had given her earlier before she'd gotten into bed.

Abby tried to haul the cover back, but the woman was stronger.

"If you want to get warm, go stand before the fire."

Sighing resentfully, Abby slid out of bed, and holding one arm across her chest and placing her other hand at the juncture of her thighs, she waddled to the fire.

Jannet set about pulling a shift over her head, and Abby helped her, thankful to be finally covered. But when Jannet tried to sit her down, Abby fought her off.

"Okay, so where are my panties?"

Jannet stared at her. "Wha?"

"Um, my underpants, um, undertrews?"

"Ye be a lass."

Abby raised her brows. "And?"

Placing her hands on her hips, Jannet leaned forward at the waist. "Ye dinnae need no trews. Ye wear a dress."

Abby realized Jannet thought she meant men's pants. "No, I mean where are my underclothes, my underpants?" When Jannet just frowned, Abby scanned the room, looking for her dirty clothes. "Where are my clothes?"

"Is that what ye call the rags ye wore? There were no pants."

Hitting her forehead with her hand, Abby tried to talk clearly as if speaking with a child. "They were small pants." She moved her hands apart to show how big and, pretending to hold a pair of panties, held her hands in front of her lower abdomen.

"Ye be talking like an *eejit*." Jannet rolled her eyes back and gazed at the ceiling as if she were thinking about what Abby said. She looked back at Abby with piercing gray eyes. "Ach, that tiny piece of rag? Aye, it's with the rest to be washed."

"Good, that's good, then. Do you have any other under-clothes I can wear?"

"Ye have yer sark."

Abby decided to leave it at that. There was no point in telling the woman about underclothes if people of that time never wore any.

The woman looked at Abby as if she were crazy. "Now sit down and let me do ye hair."

Sighing, Abby sat down, and within minutes, Jannet had Abby's hair braided and bunned with her bangs in ringlets. She pulled Abby back onto her feet and popped a beautiful satin gown over her head and buttoned up the back.

Abby took it all with good grace, her mind dipping into thoughts that Fiona MacKinnon would be at the feast. Abby wanted to look her best when she met what could very well be Iain's fiancé.

She absently played with a lock of her hair and gazed at the orb. What would happen when the MacKinnons arrived? Would the MacKinnon laird be expecting an announcement? Would Iain agree to the marriage and the joining of the clans?

Jannet nudged Abby to the long, polished metal mirror hanging on the wall, and Abby pushed thoughts of Fiona and her father out of her mind. She could do nothing about them.

She stepped in front of the mirror and gasped. The

sapphire blue of the gown matched her blue eyes perfectly. She frowned at the low neckline that seemed to increase the size of her breasts. She felt them, wondering if there was some padding under them. Nope. It was all her. She tilted her head and smiled at her reflection. She had never envisioned having an hourglass figure, but the dress showed one off in its entire splendor. She grinned. Not bad. Not bad at all.

She wondered what Iain would think of her now that she was clean and so finely attired.

A knock at the door sounded a split second before it opened. Iain stood on the threshold. Abby's heart flipped as she took in his clean clothes and shaved face. He could have been straight out of the cast of a historical movie. With his belted kilt, the white shirt that made his tanned skin seem even darker, and his ebony curls flowing over the shirt's collar, he would have been the hero for sure. HERE

She wiped her clammy hands down the sides of her dress as his eyes roamed over her from head to foot, and as they rose again, they lingered on her décolletage before spearing her eyes. Her insides dipped, and tingles ran along her backbone. Heat, red and molten, flooded her cheeks as she locked her gaze with his.

No one moved until Abby glanced at the ever-watching Jannet. The woman peered from Abby to Iain and, smashing her lips together as if she were trying not to smile, wrapped a thick scarf in the same green plaid as Iain's kilt around Abby's shoulders and ushered her to the doorway.

"You are beautiful," Iain whispered.

"So are you."

His lips quirked in a smile, but his eyes remained filled with admiration.

They had only reached the top of the stairs, when a commotion broke out below. The shouts for Iain sounded distraught.

CHAPTER 22

Iain said, "Go to yer room, and I will come and get ye later."

Abby nodded but stayed staring down at the large entrance as Iain leapt down the stairs two at a time.

A man in a green tartan and a bonnet made of the same material talked in hushed tones to Iain and Donal, Iain glancing up at Abby every now and then.

Once the messenger left, Iain ascended the stairs and smiled at Abby. "It seems the MacKinnons won't be visiting after all."

"Why?"

"Kenneth MacKinnon sends his regrets. It seems Fiona has run off with the captain of MacKinnon's guard."

Abby didn't know what to say. "I'm sorry."

"Nay, I am glad she found someone else. We wouldna have suited."

He crooked his arm, and she placed her hand on his forearm as they descended the stairs.

The buzz of voices silenced as Iain and Abby stepped into

the great hall. All eyes watched Abigail walk arm in arm with their laird to the slightly elevated front table.

Maeve stood as they approached. She was resplendent in a jade gown, her dark hair coiffured in perfect curls on top of her head. "I am pleased to see you are well rested."

Abby's back stiffened when Iain's sister never smiled at her, but she gave Maeve her most gracious smile in return. "Yes. Thanks."

A strange look passed between Maeve and Iain as they sat, Iain next to his sister and Abigail on his other side.

The serving people brought out trenchers topped with what might have been duck or some kind of wildfowl.

Everyone in the great hall ate, drank, and laughed merrily.

Abby picked at the food before her, wondering what was going on between Iain and his sister.

Trying to enjoy the festivities, Abby drank the bittersweet wine. As soon as she figured out how to work the time device, she would be gone. Without that fact hanging over her head, she would have been excited by the sounds and sights of the night. Everyone was so friendly, so happy their laird was safe. If she was born of that time, she would have joined in the merriment.

Iain and Maeve spoke of the crops and stock. He joked that a woman of Maeve's age could not keep his lands and people so healthy, and that she must have had some factor helping her.

Maeve pretended to be offended and slapped him on the shoulder. "You are an oaf, sir. I am more suited to numbers than you ever were."

Iain laughed. "That's true. I had no need of the classroom. A laird has to know how to fight, not add and spell."

Maeve grinned. "Thank goodness you are good at those things naturally, or we would all be in dire straits." She sipped her wine and then plonked her cup onto the table. "Now that ye are rid of Fiona, we must talk about who ye are to marry. Ye gave Father ye word ye would marry before yer thirty-three, and that's only weeks away."

"Aye, but we dinnae have to worry aboot that tonight."

Abby frowned. He had to marry before his birthday? She looked around the cavernous great hall at all the beautiful women making eyes at him. He wouldn't have any trouble getting someone to marry him if he had to choose from them, that was for sure, but she supposed he would have to find some other laird's daughter. From everything he had said, strengthening his clan was the most important thing to Iain.

Once the food stopped coming, the bagpipes started up.

Maeve clapped her hands together. "A reel. How marvelous. Come on, Iain, dance with your sister."

Giving Abby a longing look, he took Maeve's arm and joined the throng already on the floor.

Abby had seen reels performed, but she had never learned how to dance one. She hoped like mad that no one would ask her to dance.

Donal, his wild red hair pulled back and tied behind his head, strode over to her table, and with only her sitting there, she knew he was coming toward her. Now what was she supposed to do? *Please don't ask me to dance.*

His great hulk stood beside her and held out his hand. "Dance?"

Abby stared at his hand as if it had turned into a hairy spider. "I don't know how to dance."

Donal threw his head back and laughed. "Not dance? I thought every lass comes out of the womb knowing how to dance."

The music stopped, and Maeve was the first back to the table. "I'll have ye know, we womenfolk spend many an hour as you do perfecting our steps."

Iain joined them. "What is the problem?"

"Abigail doesn't know how to dance," Maeve said, a slight condescending smile on her lips.

"Then I will teach the lass." He held out his hand. "Come."

Frowning, Abby narrowed her eyes at him. The moment they'd stepped into his castle, he'd shifted in personality. His brogue got heavier by the second, and he wasn't as warm as he had been on the road or in the houses. When he spoke, everyone listened . . . and obeyed. "Is that an order?"

"Aye."

Without giving her a chance to decline, Iain pulled Abby out of her seat and onto the cleared floor. "Follow me and all will be well."

"Easy for you to say."

Looking around the hall, Abby's heart sped up at the many eyes watching her. She gave a slight shake of her head.

Thankfully, Iain gave some sort of silent message to the pipers, and the music slowed enough that with Iain keeping his steps simple, Abby was able to keep up. She only stepped on his feet a few times, and she saw that as a success.

He brought her back to the table, flushed and exhilarated.

"Nicely done," Maeve said, eyeing Abby warily.

Iain withdrew his arm from under Abby's hand and sat down, calling for more wine.

As they took up their cups, Alistair and another young man pushed through the great doors and hurried to Iain.

"M'lord?" Alistair said.

Iain stood up. "What is it?"

"Granny sent me. There is to be a great storm hitting us by morning. The strait will be unsailable. She thought you would like to hear the news."

"Granny was right." Iain's shoulders seemed to relax at the lad's words. "Thank her for me when next you see her."

"Aye."

"Now go and have some fun." Iain waved his arm toward the great hall.

"Thank ye, m'lord."

Frustration or impatience flashed across Donal's face. "Would you do me the honor of dancing, Abigail?"

Iain flicked his hand in the air. "Nay, she is exhausted from her travels, and it's time she retired."

Abby glowered at Iain. How dare he speak for her? He gave her an almost imperceptible look that said *don't.*

He stood up and guided her out of the great hall. Once alone at the bottom of the steps, Abby rounded on him.

"How dare you speak for me? I'll be the one to make the decision if I want to go to bed or not, not you. And don't ever silence me with a look again."

"I apologize, my sweet angel, but I could not guarantee the red firestorm's safety if he put his hands on you." His expression turned to a boyish tease. "Donal is my most skilled swordsman, and I would have hated to go into battle with him."

"Honestly?" Abby let the sarcasm drip from the word.

He closed his arms around her and chuckled. Abby put her hands against his chest to push him away, but her heart fluttered at the rumbling of his heart under her palms.

"With the storm nearly upon us, we will be safe tonight and tomorrow. God willing, we can send word to your family." Placing his fingers under her chin, he tilted her head back. "You are exhausted, my love."

Abby sighed. Iain still believed she was from his time. There was no family to send a message to. At least, not in eighteenth-century Scotland. None she knew of, that is.

Tipping her head back, she gazed at Iain. He was looking at her as if he were trying to sort out some kind of puzzle. His eyes darkened, and he bent his head, placing feathery kisses on her mouth. She didn't pull back, couldn't pull back.

She was mesmerized by the feeling stirring throughout her body. Without thought, she leaned forward, and apparently taking her movement as permission, he wrapped his arms around her and kissed her.

Pure joy flowed through her, and she kissed him back, pushing thoughts of leaving him out of her mind and reveling in the sensations his closeness caused.

When the kiss came to an end, Iain didn't let her go. Instead, he hugged her to him, her head resting on his chest. Abby listened to his heart, fast but strong and even. Her heart thumped in time to his tempo. It was as if both had merged into a beautiful waltz.

"I dinnae want to lose ye, Abigail Davis, but we must get word to yer family. They will be worried aboot ye."

He had broken the spell. She could no longer hear the music in their chests. He loosened his grip, and she automatically did the same. Once they'd separated, Abby had the strongest desire to clasp him back again. The feeling of desolation was real; it sent an ache throughout her chest.

Abby stared at him and fought the nearly uncontrollable urge to leap into his arms. In another time and place, she would jump at the chance to marry her handsome Highlander, but even if they were of the same time, she couldn't spend the rest of her life with someone who didn't believe her. Even if what she'd told him sounded ludicrous, she would want the love and support of her partner. She would want his trust, his belief in her.

A heaviness settled in her chest. She had to admit she felt more than a passing crush for the man, but there was just too much working against them, and the worst thing at that moment was that he still didn't believe her.

She pulled her hands out of his. "You don't believe me. You don't believe I came from the future." Her hands felt like sandpaper as she rubbed her face. "I guess it doesn't matter, but I have to go back."

"I do believe ye believe what ye say, lass, but until ye can recall how you got to the moor that night, we cannae find yer kin."

Abby couldn't believe what she was hearing. He hadn't heard a word she'd said. He still believed she had a grandmother in Scotland somewhere.

Her gaze rose to his eyes, and she nodded. She had to figure out how the time device worked, and she had to do it that night. If she stayed with Iain any longer, she might not ever want to go home. Her brain seemed to tilt as a raging war of possibilities filled her mind. Could she stay? Surely one little person out of time couldn't do much damage to the order of history? However, another voice argued, it would do a great deal of damage. Who knew who Iain was supposed to marry? Maybe he just hadn't met her yet.

She gazed up into his warm eyes but quickly looked away. She couldn't let herself be drawn in by them again. "I know you don't believe me, but I have to leave tonight."

She stepped on the first step and slowly climbed the stairs, her heart and legs becoming heavier with each step.

"Wait. May I look at yer treasure more closely?"

She shrugged without looking back. "If it helps you to believe me, sure."

Her mind argued with itself all the way to her door, and it seemed somehow appropriate that the moment she stepped over the threshold, a flash of lightning lit the room, followed almost immediately by a crash of thunder. The wind howled through and around the stone building. The storm was close, and her departure, imminent.

CHAPTER 23

An ache filled Iain's being at the sadness in his angel's eyes, and he realized then that he didn't want to believe her. He didn't want to contemplate she might be telling the truth. He didn't want to believe that her treasure could take her away from him.

But somehow, he knew she told the truth, and somehow, he knew then that his father's friends were from the future. Had his father known? Iain's mind traveled back to a time not long before his father had passed into the next world. Iain's father and his friends, Mark and Dianne, were sitting at the other end of the long table when Iain entered the morning room. Dianne gave Iain's father a picture, and his father laughed, nodding his head in agreement at something Mark had said. Iain's father's eyes were wet from either laughter or tears, Iain didn't know.

But he heard his father's words. "I will rest in peace knowing this will come aboot."

"Iain?" Abigail's voice brought him back.

"I'm sorry. What did ye say?"

She was holding out her treasure, the white orb with the fine artistry of leaves around the middle.

"Do you want to have a look?"

"Aye." Iain took the orb and turned it over in his hands. "It is beautiful. A skill of workmanship I have never had the pleasure of beholding before."

"I'm not sure if an artisan did it or . . ."

"Or?"

Abigail let out a breath of air. "I suppose it doesn't matter what I say. You won't believe me, anyway. A machine might have formed the leaves."

"A machine? Nay. Only a skillful hand could do such precise work."

"Not in the future. Machines can do better and more detailed work in a fraction of the time it would take a human."

It dawned on Iain how much he could learn if Abigail stayed. What other wonders waited for his people in the future? What of the English?

"Tell me, then, what happens to Scotland and her people now that the English have invaded?"

She took the orb back and studied its casing. "You'll know this soon enough anyway. See that kilt you're wearing?" Iain looked down at his dress and nodded. "They're going to be banned soon. The Dress Act of 1746 will ban the wearing of kilts or any tartan in Scotland—but don't worry, it will be repealed by 1782."

As she spoke, she kept twisting the top of the orb this way and that.

Iain didn't care about the wearing of kilts at that moment. He had the alarming thought that she would succeed in leaving him. Mark's board game from his childhood came to mind. "Wait."

Abigail stopped and gazed at him, her eyes still cloudy with sorrow.

"Please. Wait here. I want to show ye something."

He ran out of the room, shouting for Jannet. She was his and Maeve's nanny before she became a lady's maid. She would know where their toys were stored.

"Jannet!" he bellowed as he ran down the stairs.

"What are ye yelling aboot?" Jannet said from the door that led to the kitchen.

"I have to find a game, a game I had when I was a wee lad."

"All yer childhood things are in the attic." Jannet clasped his arm to stop him from leaving. Her eyes narrowed, and she tilted her head. "What are ye looking for?"

"A game Mark and Dianne gave me."

"Och, Mark and Dianne. Come this way." She turned and headed back down to the kitchen.

Iain followed. "But ye said they were in the attic."

"Aye, yer Scottish childhood things, but not anything from Dianne and Mark. Yer father's friends were very secretive, ye know."

Iain thought that if they were from the future, they had every reason to be secretive.

Jannet rushed through the busy kitchen, into the pantry, and pushed aside a large set of shelves laden with bags and bottles with ease. A heavy wooden door filled with strips of metal and with a lock made from the same type of metal stood behind the shelves.

Iain felt along the shelving unit and down the metal sides of the structure with his hands but couldn't find anything untoward, except that they were all joined together to make one piece by the strips of metal. "How?"

Jannet laughed. "Look down. See those indentations along

the floor? Mark called them rails, and although we didn't know what he was talking about, we could see the little wheels on the bottom of the *unit*. That's what Dianne called the shelves."

Iain bent down, and sure enough, there were six small wheels fastened to the underside of the shelves.

Opening the door, Jannet swept her hand before her, indicating Iain should enter first. Darkness engulfed him as he stepped over the threshold, and he blinked, trying to get his eyes used to the gloom, but then a soft warm light brightened the room somewhat.

Clothes hung from hangers on the back wall and shelves were filled with his family's keepsakes, but Iain spotted the board game on an old wooden table in the center of the room.

The room brightened and he spun around. Jannet had set a sconce on fire on either side of the now-closed door. He eyed the metal-clasped door.

Jannet smiled. "When I closed the door, the unit glided back into place on the other side."

"Why didn't ye tell me aboot this place?"

"Yer father told me to only show ye the room and its contents if ye asked about Mark and Dianne. He believed until then, ye wouldna be ready for the truth."

Walking slowly around the table as if he were stalking a deer, Iain scratched his chin. The truth of what? "That makes no sense."

"Why did ye ask aboot the game, then? Why now? Is it because of the lass ye brought into the keep?"

Iain regarded Jannet with new eyes. She had been his and Maeve's nanny, but she had also been his mother's closest confidant, and after his mother had passed into the next life, she had been his father's rock. She'd kept him going for the clan, for his children, for himself.

"Ye knew about them? Ye knew why they were different from us?"

"Aye, yer mother and father trusted me to keep their secret. Now tell me, why do ye want the game now, and where is the lass from?"

"I want to show it to her, to ask if she's ever seen the likes of it before, and I don't know where she is from, but she says she is leaving this night."

Just saying the words brought a new ache to Iain's chest.

"Does she have a white ornamental piece?"

"Aye."

Jannet's eyes widened in horror. She extinguished the lights, and the door opened. "Ye must go to her this minute."

"Are ye saying her treasure will take her away, that ye believe she is from the future?"

"Aye, I know she is, and so, too, were Dianne and Mark, they are her parents. There are many miracles in this world, my laird, and we have had the fortune to see two such marvels in our time. But ye must go. I can see ye love the lass, so stop her before she leaves ye forever." She pushed against his chest. "Go."

He did love Abigail, and he berated himself for not telling her, so he scooped up the board game and hurried through the doorway.

Racing through the castle and bounding up the stairs two and three at a time, he charged into the bedroom. Abigail was standing like an angel, the orb in her hands and a light casting a strange glow over her. "Abigail?"

She grimaced, and the light sparked against her wet cheeks. Iain's heart thudded. She was crying.

"I found out how it worked," she said.

"No. Please, Abigail, I love ye. Don't go."

"I can't stop it. I'm sorry, Iain. I love you too."

Iain was beside himself, and without thinking of the

consequences, he leapt forward and slapped the device out of her hands. Abby fell back against the wall.

Iain bent to pick up the device, but just as his fingers neared it, it disappeared.

"Uh-oh," Abigail said.

Kneeling beside Abigail, Iain took her into his arms. "I love ye."

He kissed her before she could respond, sure she would be angry at him for losing the device, for losing her only way home. He brushed his lips against hers. "I'm sorry."

She giggled and pulled back. "Don't be sorry, because I'm not. At that last minute, when you said you loved me, I would have done anything not to go home." She snuggled her head into his chest. "Thank you."

Joy exploded in Iain's chest, and his heart drummed an unnatural rhythm as a beat was missed.

"What is that?" Abigail asked, pointing to the board game that must have fallen onto the floor.

He spread out onto his stomach over the rugs, pulled the game to him, and handed it to her. "My father's friends gave it to me when I was just a wee child. Have you seen something like it before?"

"*Monopoly?* " She turned the game over in her hands and tipped her head at Iain. "Who were your father's friends?"

"Mark and Dianne were their names."

Abigail gasped and dropped the game. "Mark and Dianne? That is their names, that's my parent's names."

"Mayhap your parents and my father's friends were one in the same. They were different from Sottish people, not only because they spoke differently but the acted differently too." He smiled. "Not unlike ye."

Abigail stroked the box in her lap. "I wish they were here now." She looked up, tears glistening in her eyes. "Your father must have known they were from the future so he must have been very open minded. How did everyone get along? Can you remember?

"I remember they were friendly and all here liked them immensely."

"I hope your people like me as much then."

He pulled her up onto her feet and, bringing her in close, kissed her, enjoying the sensations she elicited in him. He spoke between depositing kisses on her lips, her jawline, her cheeks. "They will love you as I do. Will ye marry me?"

The air vibrated a hum throughout the room. Iain glanced up and blinked. Three people appeared as if out of the very air between them and the door. One man and two women, all strangely dressed and all holding the white trinket that only a moment before disappeared before his very eyes. The black-haired woman was dressed like a man, in trews.

The young blonde woman groaned. "Wow, that was weird." She looked up and screamed, "Abby!"

Abby jumped back out of Iain's arms and gasped.

He pushed Abigail behind him. "Who are ye and how did ye get into the keep?"

His gaze dropped to the orb the man was holding. "Who are ye?"

"It's all right, Iain," Abigail said as she moved around Iain and ran to the three intruders. "How did you get here? Where's Bree?"

The man held up the orb, and Abigail frowned at it as if she'd never seen it before.

The small blonde lass threw her arms around Abigail as the man spoke. "Bree stayed behind."

The small one spoke between great sobs at the same time. "Oh, Abby, we were so worried about you."

The trew-clad, dark-haired lass pulled the blonde away and gave Abigail a hearty hug. "I'm so glad you're okay."

As she spoke, she eyed Iain before her gaze went to the bed.

"Why didn't you come back with the device?" The man's voice was brusque.

The dark-haired lass laughed and nodded her head toward Iain. "I think he might have had something to do with that."

Abigail pointed to her treasure. "How did you make the orb bring you back in the exact same place I am?"

"I have no idea," the dark-haired one said. She waved a hand in the air at Abigail's confused look. "The orb just appeared on the basement bench and I picked it up. Izzy and Garrett touched it at the same time and"—she shrugged—"here we are."

The blonde lass said, "Bree said you couldn't come back without the orb. Oh, Abby, I was so worried we'd never see you again."

The man glared at Abigail. "She also said it wouldn't have come back to us unless you sent it."

"Ah, I didn't mean to. It was an accident," Abigail said.

The man huffed.

"Maybe," the dark-haired one said, "the orb is linked to the person who used it last."

"Cool, huh?" the blonde said.

Iain rubbed the palms of his hands down the sides of his face. He didn't understand anything any one of them was saying.

The blonde narrowed her eyes at the young man. "Garrett still refused to believe you'd time traveled." She beamed at Abigail. "Bet he believes it now."

"Only because I have no choice now," the man said.

Iain cleared his throat to let Abigail know he was still there.

"Oh, I'm sorry, Iain." She held out her hand, and Iain took it. "These are my sisters." She pointed to the dark-haired lass.

"Maxine." Then, to the blonde. "And Elizabeth. And the surly man there is my brother, Garrett.

"And guys? This is Laird Iain MacLaren."

"A laird, huh?" Maxine said. She regarded Iain with admiration in her eyes. "Not bad, not bad at all."

Abigail laughed. "Don't, Max. He's not used to people from the future popping up out of nowhere and talking like that."

"Come here." Garrett pulled Abigail close. "You too," he said to the lasses. "We're out of here."

Iain took a step forward but hesitated. He had no right to stop Abigail if that's what she wanted.

She twisted out of her brother's grip and ducked out of his reach. "No."

"What?"

"I said no." She turned to Iain. "Do you still want to marry me?"

"Aye. This day and forever."

She rushed into his arms. "Then I say yes, yes, this day and forever."

He silently promised that he would spend his days making sure Abigail never regretted staying with him.

CHAPTER 24

A bby couldn't believe she was saying yes to marriage, saying yes to marriage with a laird of all things. But could she stay in eighteenth-century Scotland? Should she even be contemplating it? It was one thing to say yes to spending the rest of her life being loved by her Highlander, but quite another to live the rest of her days in what to her felt like prehistoric times.

She wanted to stay in his arms, but she knew she would have to face her siblings sooner or later. "Iain, can I have some time with my family? I think we need to talk."

He kissed the top of her head. "Aye. I need to talk to my family also."

Once he'd left, Max, Izzy, and Garrett all began to talk at once. Abby let them go on for a moment, and then said, "Be quiet and let me speak."

Max stepped between Izzy and Garrett and hit them on their arms. "Let her speak."

"Thanks," Abby said, and went on to tell them all that had happened to her since arriving in eighteenth-century Scotland.

Once she'd finished, she said, "And I'm in love with Iain, and I want to stay and marry him."

"No," Garrett said, and they all stared at him. "You can't stay here. You've seen the brutality of this time." He waved a hand in the air. "And there are other things to think about. Your health, for one. What if you get sick? Are you going to let them bleed you with leeches? Give you laudanum? For Pete's sake, it's opium."

Abby shushed him with her finger on her lips. "Keep your voice down. The whole castle will hear you."

"I don't want you to stay here," Izzy said.

"Nor do I," Max said.

"Good, then that's settled," Garrett said. "Grab the orb, Abby, and let's go."

Abby plonked down on the side of the bed and rubbed her face. "Don't say anything else. Just let me think."

Tears filled her eyes. What was she to do? She couldn't just leave Iain moments after accepting his marriage proposal. A thought hit her, then. If he loved her as much as she did him, would he go back with her? But could she ask that of him? The thought of not having him in her life was just too much to bear, and she decided she could definitely ask him.

❦

Iain sat at his writing and planning table in the solar, waiting for Jannet, Maeve, and his most trusted guards, Donal and Callum. They had to accept and protect Abigail if she stayed and married him.

His heart sank with the realization that Abigail's family had come to take her away from him. They would be persuading and cajoling her into returning to their time with them right at that minute. Iain hoped she would tell him of her decision if it came to that and not just leave the castle, leave him.

Jannet arrived first, and she had a small box in her arms that she set down at the end of the table. "Och, ye have more guests."

"How do ye know that?"

"I can hear." She gave Iain a small smile and a look that said she knew a lot more than Iain had ever thought.

Iain frowned. Had she been listening at the bedroom door?

Maeve entered, with Donal and Callum a few steps behind her. All three eyed Jannet warily, and Iain had to choke back a laugh. He could almost hear their brains turning. Did Jannet tell him something they would have preferred him not to hear?

Iain stood up, went to the door, and told the guard there to fetch wine and cups. Once they were filled and handed to his four guests, he took a cup, bid the guard leave with a nod, and returned to sit behind the desk.

He raised his chalice. "A toast."

Everyone put their cups in the air.

Iain continued. "To the MacLarens and all others who abide here. May we survive the English onslaught and drive them from our lands."

"Aye," voices called out in unison.

Donal sat beside Iain, and Callum dragged a chair to the desk.

"Your lassie is a strange one," Callum said.

"Aye," Maeve said. "I have questions aboot that one."

Iain raised his brows and shot a glance to Jannet. "Questions?"

"Aye. The servants are talking. They say she is like a witch."

"She is not a witch. An angel, perhaps, but not a witch."

"I said they say she is like a witch, but without a witch's powers or standing."

"Explain."

"She speaks strangely." At Iain's opening of his mouth to say something, Maeve continued. "Yes, you said she was from the Americas, but I know people who have traveled there and back. They still speak as we speak mostly. I would not take them as not belonging in our world."

"Our world?"

Donal coughed. "She means that if she were a witch, she would not be of our world but of some magical place."

Smiling at Donal, Maeve placed her hand on Iain's arm. "Aye. And she walks strangely. She looks like she has never worn skirts before. She is always hitching the hems up and letting her legs walk freely. She has a strange aspect. I don't know what it is." She tilted her head and thought for a moment. "Her skin is smooth, but there's something aboot her eyes." She let out an impatient huff. "Oh, I don't know."

"Aye," Callum said. "It is her eyebrows. They are shaped strangely, are they not?"

"Aye," Maeve said. "Callum has the right of it. They make her whole face, ah, not wrong . . . different."

"Beautiful," Donal said.

Callum nodded his head. "Aye."

Iain let out a growl at their enraptured faces. "That is enough, ye two." He rubbed his now clean-shaven chin, missing the feel of his beard's bristles. Studying his sister and the two men he had known since they were all babes in arms —the two men he trusted above all others—he wondered if he should tell them. His gaze drifted to Jannet. She nodded in encouragement. Iain returned his attention to the three he loved above all else. Perhaps they could dispel the gossip.

Donal and Callum exchanged questioning glances over the rims of their cups.

Maeve narrowed her eyes. "What is it that is so secret you have to tell us behind closed doors?"

Iain steepled his hands under his chin. "What I am aboot to tell you will not leave this room." Maeve bit her cheek, as she was wont to do when asked to do something she didn't like. "You are not to tell a soul, Maeve, not even your maid-servant."

"But Leah and I are friends. We share all together."

"Not this time, love. Please give me your word."

She glanced at Donal, who gave a slight nod. Iain stopped the smile from forming on his lips. Donal had always been the eldest, the one Maeve would call if she couldn't get her way with Iain. He would champion her side more times than not.

Plopping back on the settee, Maeve nodded. "Aye, you have my word."

Iain stood up and walked around to the front of the table. "Abigail is not from our time. Wait. No talking until I am finished." He waited until they had stopped gazing at one another with skeptical faces. "She is from the future. That is why she talks, walks, and appears different."

Maeve folded her arms across her chest and humphed. "That is the silliest thing I have ever heard."

Donal rose and placed his arm on Iain's shoulder. "Ye really believe that?"

"Aye. I've been with her for weeks . . ." He frowned. "I am not sure, it could have been months. I was dying, and she saved my life. If it weren't for her, I would still be on the battlefield, dead."

He went on and explained about her time device. Fielding questions, he answered what he could about her time, but suggested if they had any questions, they should ask her themselves. "But make certain ye are no' overheard," he said.

Letting out a laugh, Donal said, "If she is from the future, she knows how we fare in the next battle."

"No. She knows history, but not all battles were written aboot, and much of Scotland's ballads and tales were never written. Also, remember, if Abigail hadn't appeared on the moors that day, I would have died, and Sir Thomas and his army would not have known I was alive. With her arrival, the future was already changed."

After he finished, Callum threw back his head and laughed, nearly choking on his own mirth. "Perhaps, then, she should not have saved your skin, and then the keep and lands here would have been safe from the hands of the Sassenachs."

Leaping to her feet and thumping Callum on his head, Maeve snarled, "How can ye say such a thing? Ye would prefer to see Iain dead? For him not to have come back to us?" Tears filled her eyes as she turned to Iain. "I will try to get to know your future lass." She threw herself into his arms. "I am thankful she brought ye home, brother of mine."

Callum got up, and both he and Donal slapped Iain on the back. "Aye," Callum said. "I am looking forward to killing the beasts who tried to kill our laird. You have my loyalty in this thing and in any battle."

"Thank you, Callum. I know I do." Iain grinned.

"But I cannae believe the lass is from the future. Mayhap she is, ah . . ."

"Ye mean mad?" Donal said. "Aye, my laird, I know ye have been smitten with the lass, but she cannae be from the future. 'Tis impossible."

"Not impossible," Jannet said.

Everyone watched her stand up and move to the desk as if they had forgotten she was even there.

She pulled a framed picture out of the box. It was an image of Mark and Dianne. "Do ye remember these people?"

Donal and Callum nodded.

"I do," Maeve said. "They were Father's dearest friends." She tilted her head and gazed at the picture and smiled.

"Dianne always had wee sweet treats for me." She looked at Jannet. "They were different too."

"Aye," Jannet said. "They were from the future. In fact, they were Abigail's parents."

Donal asked, "Were?"

"Aye." Jannet gazed at the picture, tears filling her eyes. "They willna be returning to Dorpol again."

Maeve put her hand over her mouth. "They are dead?" Jannet nodded. "Does Abigail know this?"

"Aye," Iain said.

Maeve frowned.

"What?" Iain asked.

"I remember Mark and Dianne. They were wonderful people and made Mother and Father happy whenever they visited. Looking back on their visits, their strange ways, I can believe they were not of our time. Can ye believe, Callum and Donal?"

"Aye," Donal said slowly, as if remembering another time. "We trusted Dianne and Mark as Laird MacLaren did, and another thing. I remember our laird telling us they had great secrets that he would tell us one day." He shook his head as if trying not to weep. "But he never got the chance."

"Aye," Callum said. "The laird was always taunting us with the things he could tell us about them, but never even giving us a small clue. I for one would never have thought they were from the future, but now that ye say it, I can see it is so." He wagged his head. "It all fits into the puzzle now."

Maeve went to Iain, placing her hands on his shoulders. "I can see Abigail means a lot to ye, Brother. Ye have succumbed to her charms and are now embroiled in her fate. What will happen to ye if she decides to leave us and return to her time?"

Iain's chest tightened at the thought. He didn't want her

to go back. He wanted her to stay with him—to wed—and to have his bairns.

Rising onto her toes, Maeve kissed his cheek. "I can see I have caused you pain."

"Abigail's family have come to take her home."

Maeve jumped back. "What? Now? We cannae allow that. Where are they?"

Iain hesitated. He didn't want a fight to break out between his family and hers. He didn't even know if he could ask Abigail to stay with him, to share the trials of what to her was the past.

He must have waited too long, because Jannet spoke up. "She is in her rooms."

Maeve spun on her heels and headed out the door.

"Wait," Iain said.

Pausing on the threshold, Maeve looked over her shoulder and raised her brows. "Do ye want her to go?"

"Nay but let me go first. I dinnae want ye to scare them into leaving." He looked at his old nanny. "Jannet?"

She got up, and Donal and Callum moved to join her.

"Nay," Iain said to Donal. "Ye and Callum wait here."

He didn't want the two brutes standing over Abigail's family. They would scare them more than his sister ever could.

Iain strode ahead of Maeve and Jannet, knocked on the door, and opened it without waiting for an answer.

"Iain," Abigail said as soon as he stepped into the solar.

He ignored her family's piercing gazes and pulled her into his arms, kissing her as if he would never taste her sweet lips again.

When they parted, Iain said, "I love ye. Would ye stay with me? Stay in my time?"

"I love you too. But would you come with me? We'd be safe in my time."

Iain bent his head and shook it. "My duty is here. My honor would be lost if I were to forsake my sister and my people. My oaths bind me to my lands and people."

"Then we're at an impasse, then."

"Aye." He crossed his arms over his chest, and his heart ached at her forlorn look.

Had he done the right thing? He looked at his sister, who sent him a thankful smile. But Donal would make a good laird, and he would look after her. Would she hate him if he left her?

"Come on, Abby, we have to go," Garrett said.

Iain put his arm around Abigail's waist, not wanting to let her go.

"Not yet we don't," Maxine said, looking at the two Scottish women. She smiled. "Hi, we're Abby's family. I'm Maxine, this is Elizabeth, and the grumpy man is Garrett."

"I am Iain's sister, Maeve MacLaren, and"—she flicked her hand for Jannet to come forward—"Jannet here was our nanny, our parents' friend, and now, our guiding hand."

Jannet laughed. "Aye, I guide, and you go the other way."

"Not all the time," Maeve said. "I am here, am I not?" She turned to Maxine and Elizabeth. "I am glad to meet ye and would love to hear stories of the future."

"You know?" Maxine asked.

"Aye, Jannet convinced us that it is true. Jannet, do ye want to show them their parents?"

"What?" Elizabeth spluttered. "You knew our parents?"

Jannet stepped forward and held out the picture. "Aye, they were constant guests of the late laird. But we haven't seen them since the Laird passed."

Maxine took the picture and gasped, Abigail hurried to look. She gazed at the picture and lifted her sight to Iain.

He smiled. "Is that them?"

Abigail nodded. "It's Mom and Dad."

Elizabeth stroked her fingers over the images. "It *is* Mom and Dad."

"Looks like it," Maxine said.

Garrett snatched the frame out of the women's hands. "Let me have a look." He eyed Jannet. "Where did you get this?"

"Yer parents gave it to Laird MacLaren a week before he passed to the other world. I was there at the time, and they and the laird entrusted me to keep it safe for when ye came here."

"They knew we would come here?" Garrett kept his eyes narrowed.

"Aye."

That was all Jannet said, but Iain had a feeling she knew more.

And Garrett must have sensed the same because he said, "What aren't you saying? What did they say about us?"

Flitting a glance in Abigail's direction, Jannet said, "That is all ye need to know right now."

Iain would learn more from Jannet but for now, it all made sense to Iain in a strange way. It was as if Abigail was fated to come to him, to be his always.

❦

ABBY WONDERED IF HER PARENTS HAD VISITED THE MacLaren Keep after the old laird died. Were they somewhere in Dorpol right at that moment? She jogged to the window and peered down at the inner buildings of the castle walls. "What if they're here right now?"

"They can't be," Izzy said. "If they were, they'd let us know."

"Not necessarily," Max said. "If they had visited at a later date, then they would know how this little problem turns out, and they wouldn't want their presence affecting the decisions Iain and Abby made today."

Clearing his throat, Garrett gazed at the picture. "And if they have seen or know of us being here, then they know they're dead. How else would we have come into possession of the orb? Actually, if they're here right now, that means two white orbs are in existence in the same place. We shouldn't be here. Fooling around with time could be dangerous." He nodded his head as if coming to a decision. "We have to go before we run into them. Now!"

Max placed her hand on his arm. "You're right, but our parents would know that, wouldn't they? So they probably have gone back already, and we're all sitting around the table eating dinner sometime in the future as we speak here."

Garrett frowned at her. "You don't know that."

Max shrugged. "No, not for sure, but I know our parents, and I think they would have guessed we would put two and two together, and they wouldn't take a chance on fudging around with our timelines."

"I agree with Max," Izzy said.

"Me too," Abby said, wondering if the picture was telling her she could stay, could marry Iain, could live happily in the eighteenth century.

Garret focused on the picture as if he were trying to read their minds. "I suppose you're right."

Izzy nudged Abby. "What are you thinking?"

Abby tried not to smile, but her mouth had its own mind. She loved her family but she loved Iain more."

Izzy gave Abby's shoulder a little slap. "I know what you're thinking. You're thinking of staying here, aren't you? Listen, Abby, I can see how much Iain loves you, but he can't be with you twenty-four seven. We've just found one another again, and I don't want to lose you." She gazed at Max. "You don't want to lose her, either, do you, Max? Who else will listen to you when you go into command mode? I won't, and I know Garrett won't, either. You need her."

Max eyed Abby, who sent her a pleading look.

Max laughed. "Actually, I think if Abby wants to stay, she should."

Nearly choking, Garrett spluttered, "What? You've got to be joking. I thought you had more sense than that, Max."

"I guess it isn't that different from falling in love in the modern world, is it, Abs?" Max tilted her head and raised her eyebrows. "For better or worse, right?"

Nodding, Abby beamed at her sister. Max would know how happy Iain made her, she knew more about Abby than anyone.

Max's gaze took in her brother and sister. "It's crazy to me, and it does feel irresponsible to let Abby stay, but what choice do we really have when that's what she wants? I can say that she needs to come back to reality, but this is her reality now. It's insane and no one would believe it, but it would be pretty difficult to separate her from it now."

Garrett crossed his arms over his chest with a huff. "I don't like it."

With tears in her eyes, Izzy said, "Max is right." She turned to Abby. "I don't want to lose you again, but I understand, and I can see you love Iain." She took Abby's hands in hers. "I'm really happy for you. I really am."

Once Izzy dropped Abby's hands, Iain moved to Abby's side, put his arm around her waist and smiled down into her eyes.

She smiled back and rested her head on his shoulder for a few seconds before realizing that her staying there didn't have to be goodbye. She snapped her head back up and widened her eyes at her siblings.

"Hey, just because I choose to live here doesn't mean you

can't visit." Abby eyed the orb in Garrett's hand. "You could come back here anytime, right?"

Garrett studied the orb. "I have no idea. I don't even know how it brought us here this time."

"But it did, didn't it? So, it could do it again," Abby said to all three, her smile radiant and her heart filled with love for all of them.

"I think we all need some time to digest all this." Izzy turned to Maeve. "Can we stay here a bit longer? Have a look around?"

Maeve looked to her brother, who said, "Aye, but we need ye to change yer clothes."

Izzy clapped her hands. "Great."

Maeve grinned at Iain and took Izzy's and Max's hands. "Come with us. Jannet will find ye something to wear." She looked Garrett up and down. "I'll hand you over to Donal, he should have something that will fit ye."

Abby knew full well Maeve was getting them all out so she and Iain could have some alone time.

She looked from sister to sister to brother. They were adults and had their own lives to live, and those lives didn't really include her. Of course, if she went back, they would see one another every now and then, but they wouldn't be living together. They would all be forging ahead with their own futures, futures that probably included marriage and children one day. But Abby knew in her heart she would never find a love like Iain again, and she couldn't for the life of her imagine marrying anyone else.

"Have fun," she called out after them. "And try to keep out of the limelight."

"Limelight?" Iain asked.

"Yeah, I don't want them becoming the center of attention. I don't think you'd like to answer all the questions your people would have about them."

As she spoke, Iain took her into his arms. Abby sighed. It felt so right being there with him, feeling his strong arms encircled around her, holding her. She hadn't thought she was lonely in her time, but being with Iain, she realized how alone she had become, that she'd never felt at home in any of the places she'd lived. Even her family home had become just another place to meet up with her siblings. But at that moment, in Iain's arms, she felt like she would never be alone again. She felt like she was at home.

Iain nuzzled her ear. "Are ye really staying?"

Tilting her head back, Abby grinned. "Aye, if ye still want me to stay."

His whole face brightened, and he brushed his lips against hers. "Now and forever, my angel. Now and forever."

⚜

ONCE HER SIBLINGS WERE DRESSED, DONAL AND CALLUM took Garrett to the fighting pit outside. When Mauve learned Max was a skilled fighter, she wanted to show Max the arms' room and great hall. Abby and Izzy roamed around with Jannet.

"I suppose it wouldn't matter if your sister were to see," Jannet said, more to herself than to Abby.

"See what?" Abby asked.

"The secret room. Now that yer staying with us, ye should know where it is and how to enter."

Izzy clapped her hands together, and sang, "Oooh, a secret room."

Abby laughed. What castle didn't have secret passageways and rooms? As they walked the halls and down the stairs, Jannet told them the history of the castle and the Orpol MacLaren clan. Abby could almost hear Izzy's mind turning over mysterious plots for her next book.

The smells of roasting meats and baking bread filling the kitchen as they passed through reminded Abby she hadn't eaten since that morning. She paused at the end of a weathered wood table and gazed at the small freshly baked, sweet cakes. The cook hurried over and handed one to her.

"Mmm, they smell good," Izzy said.

"Thank you," Abby said to the cook. "Can I have one for my sister?"

"Aye," the cook said and picking up another, handed it to Izzy.

Izzy grinned. "Thanks."

As they ate the cakes and walked into a large pantry, Abby frowned. "I wouldn't have chosen here for a secret room."

"This is the best place," Jannet said, stopping at a set of shelves. "No one comes in here except the cook and kitchen staff. They are the most loyal of all the staff."

She pushed the shelving unit to the side and opened the thick wooden door with metal clasps, pushing it inside a room.

"Neat," Izzy said, stroking the metal sides of the shelves. "I love it."

Inside, Jannet lit the light sconces and sat down on a wooden chair while Abby and Izzy perused the contents of the room.

Abby didn't know what she expected, but the room was sparse with minimal shelving, some hangers with men's and woman's clothes from different eras, and an old wooden table in the centre.

Izzy made a beeline to the clothes racks while Abby examined the table's contents. Somehow her parents had managed to bring small, twenty-first century keepsakes back in time with them. She was surprised to see some books, but Abby noticed none were about history, only fantasy fiction and herbal remedy books. Framed photographs of her parents with a barrel-chested, kilted man, and some of her and her siblings at different ages were spread over the table. Abby picked up the one of her parents and looked closely at the Scot. He must have been Iain's father, yes, the same eyes stared out at her as if he were amused that she had found him.

"Come along," Jannet said. "Abby, you and Iain can explore this room at your leisure at another time."

"Oh, I was hoping I could try on some of these clothes," Izzy said, feigning a pout.

Jannet chuckled and opened the door. "Perhaps the next time you visit." She shooed them out.

Izzy grinned at Abby. "You're so lucky. I'd love to live here."

"It's cold and drafty, and with the dogs in the great hall in the winter, smelly," Jannet said.

"Way to make me want to stay," Abby said.

Jannet linked her arm through Abby's, and whispered. "It's not that bad, but we don't want your sister staying, she has her own life to live."

CHAPTER 25

That night, Iain called for a feast and Abby was overjoyed that her sisters understood her decision to stay with her Highlander. Garrett wasn't happy, but Abby loved him all the more because of the effort he made to be gracious and get along with Iain and his men.

Word had already gotten around that Iain and the strange woman were to marry, and many came up to his table and congratulated him. The women seemed to be a bit wary of Abby, but they nevertheless welcomed her into the clan.

The celebration feast was in full swing, and while Maeve sat on Iain's left side, Abby happily sat on his right gazing around the great hall. She had a lot to learn, but with Iain by her side, she was eager to do whatever she had to do to become accepted by his people.

Iain's table on the dais had been set to allow room for Abby's family to sit along the opposite side. Izzy claimed the seat facing Abby, and Garrett sat opposite Maeve. Max was opposite Iain.

Soft music filled the room from the players of bagpipes and flutes.

Compared to the raucous jubilation of Iain's warriors and crofters, her sisters and brother were subdued, Garrett especially, but she noted that didn't seem to hamper his hunger for food or wine.

The warriors kept glancing at the strangers at Iain's table, and Abby didn't have to hear their conversations to know what was being said. Who were those people? They acted differently, talked differently.

Thankfully, they wouldn't be saying they dressed differently, because Jannet and Maeve had dressed them in clothes of the time. Izzy looked beautiful in a jade-green gown, and she didn't mind in the least that the square neckline was cut so low. Her hair had been curled into ringlets, most of which were piled high on her head, leaving the remaining tendrils encompassing her sweet, doll-like face.

Max kept pulling at her lemon-yellow gown as if trying to give her more room to breathe. Abby smiled when one side of the MacLaren tartan she had worn over her shoulders to hide the low-cut neckline fell. Max hissed and threw the end back over her shoulder.

Garrett's nine-yard tartan showed his physique off to its best. His white shirt was a bit tight, but that only made him look more handsome. He was naturally more muscle than fat, but even though he hauled his paintings around from show to show, his muscles had gained more definition since she'd last seen him, like he'd been working out—hard.

The air around Abby tingled, and she snapped her head in all directions. Leaning forward, she whispered, "Did you feel that?"

They all shook their heads. "What is it?" Iain asked.

The serving staff flitted around the table, all ears, Abby was sure. She waited until they left and everyone in the room was busy eating. "Nothing. I'm probably a bit jittery is all."

"Ye are having second thoughts?"

"No." She smiled into Iain's eyes. "Never."

Garrett put his cup down. "Why not bring Iain and Maeve back to the future with us?"

Abby turned to Iain and gave a little shake of her head. They'd had that conversation, and she was happy with their decision. His shoulders relaxed, and he took her hand in his and kissed her knuckles.

Abby regarded Maeve's shocked expression. "Nay, I don't want to go. I have my friends here. My place is by Iain's side until I myself am wed."

Garrett let out a breath of air. "Forget it, then. I was just trying to give you a choice."

"There is no choice as far as I'm concerned. We canna leave. Our people need their laird, and now that the contract is sent to the victorious king of England, we will be left alone to tend our lands. Although the days ahead will not be without trials, we will prosper."

Iain pierced Abby with his dark eyes and gave a quick wink. "I have word that Bonnie Prince Charles is in hiding and will make it safely to France."

Heat rose on Abby's cheeks at Max's raised brows, and she shrugged, throwing her sister a wry look.

"Mayhap it is for the benefit of all Scottish people he stays there and never return to Scotland," Iain continued. "However, for those Scots who remain, many will either go or be sent to the Americas and even Australia. Some will stay in the cities of Scotland, and there will be major economic growth in our lifetime."

He squeezed Abby's hand. "I want to be a part of that growth."

"I, for one, understand that," Max said.

"Well, I don't," Garrett said.

The music sped up and increased in volume. Serving men and women began moving the tables to the walls, and Iain's most trusted men started making their way to Iain's table, shouldering one another out of the way to get to Izzy and Max's chairs first.

Young Alistair was the first to Izzy. "Would ye like to dance?"

Giving him a wide smile, Izzy shrugged. "Why not? But I have to tell you, I don't know how to dance Highland style."

She stood up and let him lead her to the now-cleared floor.

Donal and Callum approached Max at the same time. Donal bowed. "If you would be so kind, m'lady?"

Callum nudged Donal aside. "He's got two left feet, m'lady. It's me ye want to try first."

Grinning at them both, Max said, "Sorry, boys, but I'm still talking with my sister."

"It's all right, Max." Abby grinned. "You go have some fun."

Max gave her sister a look that said *no way*.

Abby laughed. "One dance won't kill you."

"How do you know?"

"Call it a hunch."

Max banged her cup down. "Fine." She stood up, and Donal and Callum backed away to give her room. She pointed to Donal. "You asked first."

A smile spread over Donal's face, twisting into a smirk as he glanced at Callum.

Abby noted while they were arguing, Garrett had taken Maeve onto the floor. Maeve twisted her head about to watch Donal and Max, and Abby was certain her new sister-in-law's eyes narrowed at the pair. Garrett pulled her arm and she quickly faced him with a smile, though to Abby, it looked forced. Garrett said something and Maeve shook her head, a wider, truer smile spreading over her lips. She took Garrett's hand and proceeded instructing him how to dance.

Their laughter sang over the crowd and Abby let out a breath. She wanted nothing to spoil that marvelous day, and she wanted her siblings to enjoy their time in the past, Abby's new forever time.

Standing up, Iain kept Abby's hand in his. "A dance, my angel?"

"Now and forever." Abby melted into his arms.

She'd never been so happy. She couldn't wait to marry Iain and spend the rest of her life with him. Oh, she knew it wouldn't be the easiest of lives, not without the comforts she was used to. She smiled into his shoulder. She intended to invent some comforts. Who knew? Maybe she was the one to introduce day spas to Scotland.

EPILOGUE

Abby gazed out the new library window across the gray, choppy waters that separated her new home from mainland Scotland. Although it was summer and the sun had fought its way through the clouds, she still hadn't become acclimatized to the cold.

She pulled her cloak around her body. It was the same cloak she had arrived in eighteenth-century Scotland in, and she loved its warmth and viewed it as her connection to her past life and family.

Absentmindedly, she readjusted her kertch, the linen headpiece that signaled to all that she was a married woman. The kertch grounded her, reminded her of her new life, and what a great life it had turned out to be. She loved Iain, and he was a thoughtful husband and partner.

So much had changed during the last year. The men had stopped wearing kilts, but Abby couldn't wait until they made a comeback. She liked Iain wearing his. The biggest thing was that Iain remained ruler of his clan, and his property wasn't sold as many others were. The fact that he did not commit his army to the rebellion was looked upon well, and although he himself fought, only Thomas was aware of that, and he was killed in France that same year.

She sighed. More changes were still to come.

A pair of arms wrapped around Abby's waist. She gasped. She knew who it was but strained her head back to look anyway.

He turned her around in his arms, his intent gaze piercing her soul. He still took her breath away with his very touch. "Ye looked sad."

"Sad? No. I was just thinking how much has happened since we met, and I can't for the life of me imagine my life any different."

"Ye dinnae want ta go back to ye family?"

"I miss them, sure, but we were all going our separate ways, living thousands of miles apart before we found the orb, so this is no different, and anyway, my *family* is here." She wrapped her arms around his neck and rested her head on his shoulder, breathing in his spicy scent.

He moved back and stroked her cheek, sending ripples of electricity through her core.

"I know ye, and ye have something on yer mind."

She bent her head, gazed at him through her lashes and smiled coyly.

"Ye do have something to tell me."

"I do."

"And when will ye be ready to do that?"

"Now."

His lips twitched. She knew he was trying to remain cool and not say anything too soon. Stretching out the moment, she flicked an imaginary piece of fluff from his shoulder.

"Tell me."

"Things are going to change a lot around here soon."

"Aye? How?"

She took his hand and placed it on her stomach, and he chuckled. "Ye are having a babe."

"*We* are having a baby."

He clasped her waist, picked her up, and spun her around, laughing and shaking his head. "We are having a babe."

Abby laughed. "Put me down."

He did. "I'm sorry. Did I hurt ye?"

"Not in the least. I was getting dizzy is all."

He moved his hands up her back and drew her in close to his chest. "Are ye happy?"

"I am happier than I have ever been." He smiled, and she frowned. "Although . . ."

His smile vanished. "What is troubling ye?"

"Nothing much. I've been thinking, though. There's not a lot for me to do here, and once word gets out about the baby, no one will let me do anything harder than sewing a pair of trousers. There are some things I miss from my time." His face became strained, and she hurried on so as not to cause him any more discomfort. "I mean, what would you say to me teaching anyone who wants to learn some futuristic pampering?"

He tilted his head and speared her with a look. "Like what?"

"Massages, hot baths, facials, stuff like that."

"I dinnae know what facials are, but I dinnae want ye massaging anyone else."

She laughed. He did like that particular skill. "Not me. We'll have men learn to massage men and women for women. Would that be acceptable?"

Small wrinkles formed at the corners of his brown eyes as he smiled. "Aye, that would be most acceptable, but how will ye teach such things without raising suspicions? I dinnae want anyone thinking ye are a witch."

"I'll handle any questions, don't worry."

"If I could give you the world, my angel, I would in a heartbeat. Ye can do anything ye want."

She hugged him. "Thank ye."

Chuckling, he put his fingers under her chin and lifted her head so he could gaze into her eyes. Her heart fluttered, and before she could take a breath, his mouth was on hers, and he kissed her like his very life depended on it.

He began to withdraw, and she held his head in place. She wasn't finished yet.

When they finally came apart, they made eye contact. "I love ye," he said.

Abby's chest exploded in tremors of excitement. "I love ye."

They wrapped their arms around one another and kissed again.

FROM CALLIE

Thank you so much for reading *From Suits to Kilts*!
Book II in The Time Orb Series, *From Bars to Ballrooms*, can
be found at your preferred store.

Want some *From Suits to Kilts* free bonus stories?
I made a book that includes what was happening in the
present time with Max, Izzy, Garrett and Bree, and a second
epilogue for Abby and Iain.

You can grab the book when you subscribe to my newsletter.
Just pop this link into your browser and let me know where
to send them:
https://www.subscribepage.com/m1n2t8

I value our friendship and will never share your email, ever.
And don't worry if you have already joined my mailing list
because all the bonuses and free books will be added to my
newsletter as I write them.

Callie's Books

The Time Orb Series:

Book 1 - From Suits to Kilts

Book 2 - From Bars to Ballrooms

Printed in Great Britain
by Amazon

22287851R00128